Bello

T0316212

hidden talent rediscovered!

Bello is a digital only imprint of Pan Macmillan,
established to breathe new life into previously published,
classic books.

At Bello we believe in the timeless power of the imagination,
of good story, narrative and entertainment and we want to use
digital technology to ensure that many more readers
can enjoy these books into the future.

We publish in ebook and Print on Demand formats
to bring these wonderful books to new audiences.

About Bello:

www.panmacmillan.com/imprints/bello

About the author:

www.panmacmillan.com/author/paulsomers

Paul Somers

Paul Somers is the pen name of Paul Winterton (1908–2001). He was born in Leicester and educated at the Hulme Grammar School, Manchester and Purley County School, Surrey, after which he took a degree in Economics at London University. He was on the staff of *The Economist* for four years, and then worked for fourteen years for the *London News Chronicle* as reporter, leader writer and foreign correspondent. He was assigned to Moscow from 1942–5, where he was also the correspondent of the BBC's Overseas Service.

After the war he turned to full-time writing of detective and adventure novels and produced more than forty-five books. His work was serialized, televised, broadcast, filmed and translated into some twenty languages. He is noted for his varied and unusual backgrounds – which have included Russia, newspaper offices, the West Indies, ocean sailing, the Australian outback, politics, mountaineering and forestry – and for never repeating a plot.

Paul Winterton was a founder member and first joint secretary of the Crime Writers' Association.

Paul Somers

OPERATION
PIRACY

BELL

First published in 1958 by Collins

This edition published 2012 by Bello
an imprint of Pan Macmillan, a division of Macmillan Publishers Limited
Pan Macmillan, 20 New Wharf Road, London N1 9RR
Basingstoke and Oxford
Associated companies throughout the world

www.panmacmillan.com/imprints/bello
www.curtisbrown.co.uk

ISBN 978-1-4472-2099-2 EPUB
ISBN 978-1-4472-2098-5 POD

Copyright © Paul Somers, 1958

The right of Paul Somers to be identified as the
author of this work has been asserted in accordance
with the Copyright, Designs and Patents Act 1988.

Every effort has been made to contact the copyright holders of the material
reproduced in this book. If any have been inadvertently overlooked, the publisher
will be pleased to make restitution at the earliest opportunity.

You may not copy, store, distribute, transmit, reproduce or otherwise
make available this publication (or any part of it) in any form, or by any means
(electronic, digital, optical, mechanical, photocopying, recording or otherwise),
without the prior written permission of the publisher. Any person who does
any unauthorized act in relation to this publication may be liable to
criminal prosecution and civil claims for damages.

The Macmillan Group has no responsibility for the information provided by
any author websites whose address you obtain from this book ('author websites').
The inclusion of author website addresses in this book does not constitute
an endorsement by or association with us of such sites or the content,
products, advertising or other materials presented on such sites.

This book remains true to the original in every way. Some aspects may appear
out-of-date to modern-day readers. Bello makes no apology for this, as to retrospectively
change any content would be anachronistic and undermine the authenticity of the original.
Bello has no responsibility for the content of the material in this book. The opinions
expressed are those of the author and do not constitute an endorsement by,
or association with, us of the characterization and content.

A CIP catalogue record for this book is available from the British Library.

Visit **www.panmacmillan.com** to read more about all our books
and to buy them. You will also find features, author interviews and
news of any author events, and you can sign up for e-newsletters
so that you're always first to hear about our new releases.

Chapter One

That morning there was an unaccustomed air of lethargy about the office of the London *Daily Record*. A mid-August heat wave had just started, and at ten past eleven when I arrived the thermometer by the commissionaire's box was already registering in the upper seventies. Normally there would have been a sprinkling of callers by now, but to-day the visitors' benches were empty. Sergeant Stubbins, the most correct of commissionaires, had discarded his ribboned jacket and was sitting back in his shirt sleeves reading the *Record's* sports page. He gave me a limp nod as I entered and handed me the key of the Reporters' Room, which meant I was the first arrival. I took the lift up. The Reporters' Room smelt of stale smoke and dust. I flung all the windows wide open and switched on the big electric fan that hung from the ceiling and went into the News Room to say "Good morning" to Blair, the News Editor.

Blair enjoyed heat, and he seemed in an amiable mood. I didn't need to ask him if there was anything doing, because there obviously wasn't. The small pile of agency copy that had accumulated during the night had already been sorted and dealt with. The tape machines were silent. The copy boy, whose job it was to tear off the tape, was reading a comic. Blair's secretary was cleaning the letters of his typewriter. Blair himself had his black box out, a sure sign that the news front was lifeless. The black box contained dossiers on old story possibilities that hadn't matured, and when Blair couldn't find anything else for his reporters to do he'd pass them around and get us to bring the inquiries up to date. He was thoughtfully sifting through them now. Martin, a Jekyll-and-Hyde character who was sometimes a reporter and sometimes a Deputy Assistant News Editor, was at the other side of the desk, quietly perusing the latest batch of entries for the *Record's* silly-season competition—"What would you do if you had £5,000?" It was all very peaceful—like the eye of a hurricane.

As I returned to the Reporters' Room, Jack Lawson came in. Lawson was one of the Crime Reporters—a slim, pale, jaunty man of thirty or so. He said, "Morning, old boy—bloody hot, isn't it?" and took a letter from his pigeon hole. He glanced at the hand-writing, winced, and tore it up without opening it. "Women!" he said. Lawson was always having woman-trouble. He tossed the bits into a waste basket and went into the News Room to report.

Smee was the next to arrive. Smee was a big, shambling man, flat-footed and fifty-ish. He looked, in Lawson's phrase, like "a worn-out cop". On a story, he was plodding and competent. In the office he had a perpetually hurt expression, like an animal that has been kicked around a lot and doesn't know why. He muttered something about the heat, stuck his head in the News Room door, withdrew it quickly in case someone should give him a job, and walked over to his desk.

I said, "What was Hatcher so mad about last night, Bill? You seemed to be having a frightful row." Hatcher was the Night News Editor, a bullying type with a barrack room manner.

"He tried to make out I was late back from supper," Smee said, wiping the sweat from his forehead. "He's always after me for something. I'll get that bastard one of these days, you see if I don't." He opened a drawer, and took out the sheaf of papers and the bottles of coloured inks that he used for his complicated racing system and started to work on it. He looked happier at once.

Lawson returned, glanced at the duty list, said, "Why is it we always have a high-powered staff on when there's no news?" and sat down to do his expenses.

After a moment or two, Hunt came in. Hunt was the Chief Reporter—a handsome, middle-aged, immaculately-dressed man, confident and ebullient.

"There's a woman at the front box with a pram, asking for Mr.

Lawson," he said, looking as pleased with himself as though he'd just made the crack for the first time. He opened the News Room door, called "'Morning, Blair!" in an off-hand way and went to his desk. He took a clothes brush from a drawer and began to brush his impeccable trouser bottoms.

Lawson said, "Your turn to buy the coffee, Fred."

"I bought it yesterday," Hunt said indignantly. "Smee'll buy it—he's always in the money."

"I haven't had anything come up for days," Smee said.

"Well, there's nothing like a generous action to bring you luck. Come on, Smee, do your stuff—I'll have mine black."

Smee made a vaguely grumbling noise, reached for the desk telephone, and dialled the canteen for four coffees.

Hunt looked over Lawson's shoulder, studying his expenses sheet. "'Hospitality, £47s. 6d.'", he read out, and gave a loud guffaw. "You'd better watch your step, Jack. The Editor's started an economy drive."

"What, again?" Lawson said, tapping away.

"This time it's serious. Didn't you hear about Ridley?"

"No."

"Why, he had Ridley on the mat yesterday and made him explain each item in detail. Slashed everything to ribbons, I'm told."

"Really?" Lawson said, looking worried.

"That's right," Hunt said, enjoying himself. "Even scored out 'Glass of milk, 5d.' Said he didn't believe Ridley had ever had a glass of milk in his life."

"Good lord!" Lawson pondered. "Oh, well—better play it safe, I suppose." He began tapping again. I joined Hunt behind him. He'd struck out the item £4 7s. 6d. and substituted £2 10s. 8d. "Pity they can't trust us," he said.

The News Room door suddenly opened with a bang and the copy boy came out, whistling shrilly between his teeth, and dumped an enormous pile of competition entries in front of Smee. "Mr. Blair says you're to pick the winner," he said with a grin, and departed.

Hunt said, "What would you do with £5,000, Smee?"

"He'd hire a couple of assassins to slit Hatcher's throat," Lawson said.

Smee looked disgustedly at the pile of papers. "You know, I read through three hundred of these bloody things yesterday."

"You *read* them!" Lawson said, in a shocked tone. "Haven't you ever heard of automation, old boy? Look, let me show you." He left his typewriter, picked up the pile of papers, stood on a chair, and held them under the electric fan. For a moment he and Smee were lost sight of in a whirl of flying entries. When only one paper was left, Lawson stepped down. "Here's the winner—Mrs. Stokes of Dartford. Good for her!" He put it on Smee's desk. "You've got to keep abreast of the times, old boy—no good living in the past."

"Now I've got to pick them all up," Smee grumbled.

Hunt said, "Well, you young fellows can stew here all day if you like, but I'm going to find myself a nice out-of-town job. Something by the sea." He opened a copy of a south coast local paper and began to study it.

Presently the boy came out again and gave me a visitor's slip from the front box. A "Miss P. Bellamy" wished to see the Editor about a story. I went down to the box. An attractive young woman was waiting on one of the leather seats. She looked the sort of girl who *might* have a good story. I hoped she had, because I could certainly use one. I glanced at Sergeant Stubbins, who gave a warning headshake. I approached Miss Bellamy and said the Editor was busy, and could I help. She gave me a card, and explained that she was in tele-pathic communication with the planet Venus and had learned some Venusian tunes which she'd like us to publish. I said we never published music, but she said these were quite exceptional tunes and she was sure we'd like them. She put a hand on my arm and came close to me and began to hum a tune that sounded to me like the Blue Danube, gazing all the time into my eyes. It took me about five minutes to get rid of her, and by the time I got back to the Reporters' Room the day seemed hotter than ever.

Lawson looked up from his typewriter. "What was she like, old boy?"

"Dotty, I'm afraid." I showed him the card.

"'The Girl from Venus,'" he read out. "H'm!—sounds promising. Telephone number, too." He slipped the card into his pocket.

After a moment or two the waitress came in with the coffee. Her name was Mabel, and she had the sort of figure that looks good even in uniform. She'd only been working for the *Record* for three days.

Hunt said, "Getting used to things here, Mabel?"

"Yes, thank you," she said.

"Shaping up nicely, I'd say," Lawson said.

"Very nicely," Hunt agreed.

"What do you think, Fred?—36-24-35?"

"You've got a nerve," Mabel said, and distributed the cups.

"If you have any trouble with these reporters," Hunt said, "just come to me."

The outer door banged again as the copy boy re-emerged to tell Lawson that Blair wanted him. Lawson disappeared into the News Room. When he came out he looked distinctly peeved.

"What's happening?" I asked.

"The Editor wants a round-up on vice in the West End," he said. "A *round-up*!—and eighty-five in the shade. Wants it to-day, too."

"Oh, well," I said, "you'll only have to reminisce a bit."

"Very funny, old boy. Anyway, here's something to take the smile off your face. With Blair's love." He threw a bundle of papers from the black box on to my typewriter.

I picked up the top one. It was yellow with age, and the corners were dog-eared and frayed. I knew its contents by heart. A chap named Fowler had been planning a treasure-hunting expedition to the Sargasso Sea in a ketch, as far back as 1954, but he'd never got around to starting. The top paper of the dossier was filled with one-line memos by different reporters—"No date yet"—"No decision taken yet"—"Fowler says he'll ring us when he has anything"—all initialled. I went to one of the phone booths ranged along the wall and put in a call to Fowler. It was stifling in the box, even with the door open. There was no reply, and I went back to my desk.

As I sat down, Hunt suddenly gave a satisfied exclamation and looked up from his paper. "Now here's a good story," he said. "Camber, Sussex. Just the place for a hot day, too."

"Someone seen a mermaid?" Lawson said hopefully.

"Strange marks in the sand. A complete circle, as though a body had been dragged around, but no footmarks leading to it."

"Probably the Loch Ness Monster come south," Lawson said. "I bet you can't sell that one to Blair."

"What do you bet?"

"Glass of milk, old boy."

"Done!" Hunt got up and took his paper into the News Room. The talk behind the glass partition soon grew lively. Hunt was a redoubtable arguer when he wanted something, and he wanted a day by the sea very badly. I could see Blair grinning. There were no flies on Blair, and of course he always had his way in the end. To-day, though, he was in a mellow mood and open to persuasion. Ten minutes passed. Then Hunt came out and picked up his hat.

"You owe me a glass of milk, Jock," he said. "So long—I'll think of you poor devils toiling over your grubby slips of paper while I'm having a swim." He went out.

"Well, what do you know!" Lawson said. "The things he gets away with! Makes your blood boil."

"Mine's already boiled dry," I said.

For a moment Lawson gazed thoughtfully out of the window. Then he closed his desk. "I think I'll go along to the Yard and get the latest dope," he said. "Anything's better than staying in this oven. See you on the ice!" He went out, too.

I picked up another black box dossier. It was about a man who'd learned from a planchette that he'd die before September, and had believed it. The top page was covered with memos saying. "Still alive", with signatures and dates.

I sighed, and looked at Smee. He'd retrieved most of the competition entries from the floor and had begun to read through them. As far as jobs were concerned I thought he had the edge on me, but it was very moot. The day seemed to hold little promise for either of us.

Then, suddenly, there was an eruption in the News Room. I

could hear Blair talking agitatedly to Martin. His relaxed air had quite vanished. After a moment he came bustling out with a bit of copy in his hand. He was a short, square, very powerful man, and he bore down on me like a bulldozer.

"Curtis," he said, "will you get down to Falmouth right away?" He thrust the copy into my hands. It was an agency flash, and it said: BRUCE ATTWOOD'S YACHT WANDERER PUT BACK HERE EARLY TO-DAY AFTER BEING SUBJECTED ARMED ATTACK ON HIGH SEAS.

"Good lord!" I said.

"It may be some publicity hoax," Blair said, "but we can't take a chance. If it's true, it sounds like the story of the year."

Chapter Two

I grabbed a time-table and looked up the trains from Paddington. The eleven-thirty had gone, and the one-thirty wouldn't get me down much before nine. I could do it more quickly by car, I decided, and that way I wouldn't have any transport difficulties when I got there. I drew twenty pounds from the cashier, collected my Riley from the office garage, and was away just before noon.

The journey was uneventful, but gruelling. I knew I had to step on it if I was going to get a story back to the paper that night, and I gave the Riley all she'd got, which was plenty. The A 30 highway was fairly busy with holiday traffic, but it wasn't like a week-end, and with only a couple of brief stops for snacks at roadside cafés I managed to keep up an average of forty and still live.

On the way down, I mentally pieced together what I knew of Bruce Attwood. It amounted to quite a bit, for his name was a household word all over the country and hardly a week went by without his activities making headlines. He was a business man and a reputed millionaire—a flamboyant, larger-than-life character who enjoyed being discussed by the newspapers and had never been known to turn a reporter away without an interview. He had a very attractive wife named Charmian, a former model much younger than himself, on whom he doted to the point of making a public exhibition of himself. In his eyes she could do no wrong—there'd been an incident a few months back, I recalled, when he'd got into trouble for punching the driver of a car that she'd crashed into from behind because she wasn't looking. Charmian was even more flamboyant than he was. I associated her in my mind exclusively with lavish parties, champagne, jewels and clothes. There was one particular interview I remembered, when she'd told some newspaperman that what she stood up in was worth £70,000. She and her husband did a good deal of cruising in their Luxury yacht *Wanderer* and according to a gossip paragraph I'd read a day or two before, they'd been about to sail to the Mediterranean in her, with guests, to attend some festival at Cannes. It was a most promising background for a story, and the nearer I got to Cornwall the more excited I felt about my assignment.

I reached Falmouth just before eight. Even at that hour, the grey, granite town was packed with holiday-makers, blocking the pavements, gazing into shop windows, milling around in cars. The car park in the main square was full and it took me a little time to find an empty bit of kerb. Then a passer-by directed me to the harbour, and I slung my binoculars over my shoulder and walked quickly through the square to the Prince of Wales Pier.

One glance at the scene there was enough to tell me the story was no hoax. The pier was crowded with eager sightseers, all looking and pointing in the same direction. A police radio car was parked just outside the turnstiles, and there were more uniformed policemen on the pier itself. I paid my threepence and squeezed through the throng. I couldn't get to the railing, but my extra inches gave me a good view over the heads of the crowd. There was a fine expanse of sheltered blue water, with attractive hills half a mile ahead across the estuary. To the right, I could see docks and some large oil tankers and the channel out to the Carrick Roads. The yacht anchorage lay to the left, well off the fairway. There were boats there of every description, scores of them—dinghies and half-decked day-sailers, sloops and ketches, "fifty-fifties" and cabin cruisers, some at mooring buoys and some at anchor. A few of them were expensive-looking jobs, but only one really stood out—a very smart, white-hulled motor ship of perhaps a hundred and fifty tons, which I hadn't a doubt was *Wanderer*. A couple of launches were tied up alongside her gangway, and one of them looked like a police boat. I turned my glasses on the yacht but I couldn't see any movement aboard her. All the movement came from the dozen or so rowing boats manoeuvring slowly around her, some of them occupied by men with cameras. It looked as though the local reporters were still waiting for a break. I'd obviously have to get out there myself, but first I wanted to pick up what information I could ashore.

A large police sergeant was standing alone in a small oasis of empty pier and I elbowed my way through to him, not without some nervousness. I was still new enough in the reporting game to find uniformed authority a bit daunting at the start of a story and the sergeant didn't look as though he was exactly bubbling with bonhomie. Probably he'd had quite a day with the crowds. I almost wished Lawson was around—he had an ingratiating "old boy" technique with the police that nearly always worked. I had no technique at all—just a direct approach.

I said, "'Evening, Officer," and produced my Press pass. 'I'm Curtis of the *Record*."

"Yes, sir?" He was very polite and very stolid. If I'd said I was Sanders of the River I don't think he'd have batted an eyelid.

"Er—what's the position?" I said.

He looked at me appraisingly for a couple of seconds and then, to my surprise, he became quite friendly and told me what he knew. It wasn't very much, but it was certainly sensational. *Wanderer*, it appeared, had put to sea the previous evening, bound for the South of France. She'd returned to harbour around dawn with a report that she'd been stopped and boarded by men with guns. Attwood's secretary, a man named Scott, had been shot dead during the raid. The police, headed by a Superintendent Anstey of the local C.I.D., together with various naval and harbour officials, had been to-ing and fro-ing all day, taking statements. Scott's body had been removed to the mortuary that afternoon. Except for officials, no one had yet come ashore from the yacht, and so far no statement had been made by anybody. "They've all been too busy," the sergeant said.

I said I was sure they had. I felt relieved—at least it looked as though I hadn't missed anything. "Well," I said, "I suppose I'd better get out there, too, if all the boats haven't been taken."

The sergeant nodded. "If I were you, sir, I'd go along to the Customs Quay—you're more likely to get one there than here. That's the quay, just behind those tugs. Go up Market Street and bear to your left.

I thanked him warmly, and passed quickly through the turnstile. As I walked up Market Street, the holiday crowd grew thinner, and at the Customs Quay itself there was only a scattering of people. The little harbour, there, scarcely more than a pool, was crammed with dinghies, floating now on the high tide. Many of them were yacht tenders, but a man in a blue jersey with the word "Seagull" embroidered on it soon picked me out a hire boat and, when he learned I was a reporter, said I could use it as long as I wanted and settle up when I'd finished with it. That suited me perfectly.

It took me only a few minutes to row out to *Wanderer*. The fleet of small boats hanging around her seemed to have grown. I scrutinised their occupants carefully, but I didn't recognise anyone from London. I had a few words with a photographer from one of the West Country papers, but though he'd been there most of the day he knew no more than I did. He looked pretty browned off, and so did the others. I rested on my oars and considered what to do. I thought Attwood was almost certain to say something that evening, even if the police didn't, but I might be wrong, and if I was I'd need all the scraps of information I could get. I rowed in close to *Wanderer's* gangway and asked a bleak-looking, flat-capped policeman in the launch if he knew when we might be getting a statement, and he said he had no idea. I rowed on round the yacht, making mental notes about her in case I had to fall back on a descriptive piece. She was a little smaller than I'd first thought, but beautifully kept and obviously very luxurious inside. I could hear a murmur of voices from inside the saloon, but the curtains were drawn over the windows so that it was impossible to see anything. She looked very placid, lying quietly at anchor in the still water, and it was hard to believe she'd been the object of a violent raid only a few hours before.

After a moment or two I switched my attention to the other craft that were lying near her in the anchorage. What I needed was a quotable interview with somebody, and they seemed to offer the best hope. I let the dinghy drift slowly down on the falling tide while I took a look round. There was a ketch named *Morna*, of about ten tons, tied up to a mooring buoy a few yards astern of *Wanderer*, but she seemed to be unoccupied. Abreast of her there was a small sloop named *Wings* with a man and a girl aboard, but it turned out they'd only just arrived at the anchorage and knew nothing. Astern of her was a 40-foot motor cruiser named *Curlew*, a rather battered job in urgent need of a coat of paint. Two men in open-necked shirts and khaki shorts were sitting drinking beer in the large after cockpit—a slim, tanned one, and a pink, tubby one. A fishing rod stuck out over the stern. I called out, "Have you been here all day?" and one of them replied, "We've been here three days, on and off." They sounded quite promising interviewees. I closed up to them, grabbed hold of their counter, and introduced myself.

"Hugh Curtis?" the slim man said. "Oh, yes—I've seen your name in the paper. I take the *Record* myself, as a matter of fact ..." His tone was interested, and I congratulated myself on having hit on a regular reader. That always helped.

He glanced across at *Wanderer*. "I suppose you've come down about the raid. Pretty shocking business, isn't it?"

I agreed that it was. "Not that I know much about it, yet," I said. "Have you heard anything?"

"Only that she was attacked during the night and the old boy's secretary was shot. I guess everyone knows that by now, though."

I nodded. "Were you here when she came in this morning?"

"Yes—right here. It was about six o'clock—I was just making the tea."

"I should think you were surprised to see her back, weren't you?"

"I certainly was, after all the fuss there'd been about her trip."

"What happened after she came in?"

"Well, there was a hell of a commotion on board—raised voices, people rushing around, really quite a flap. They were in a tremendous hurry to lower their tender and I thought perhaps someone had been taken ill and they needed a doctor. Then the police arrived, and we realised there was more to it than that."

"Who fetched the police?"

"One of the crew—short, thickset chap, with fair hair."

"What about the secretary who was shot—did you ever see him?"

"Oh, yes, we saw him once or twice—but never very close. He was a young fellow, husky build, dark—that's about all I can tell you."

"Do you happen to know who else was aboard?"

"Well, the crew, of course—three men and a boy, we saw—and Attwood and his wife—and at least two others. Another man and a woman."

"You've no idea who they are?"

"Not a clue, I'm afraid." The slim man gave a faint grin. "Bit out of our class, you know—we weren't invited to any of their parties . . . Sorry I can't be more helpful."

"Oh, well, you've given me a line or two," I said. "Have you any objection to my quoting you—about seeing *Wanderer* come in?"

"Not if you don't embroider things too much! My name's Thornton—John Thornton. This is Tony Blake . . . When will the stuff be appearing?"

"To-morrow morning—that is if we use it. It'll depend what else I can get, of course. Thanks a lot, anyway."

"You're welcome."

I let go of the counter and rowed slowly back through the anchorage. The armada of waiting dinghies was still growing and by now I recognised one or two familiar Fleet Street faces among their occupants. Attwood was going to have a good audience for his story when he finally broke silence. But the police were still aboard the yacht, and there wasn't a sign of anything happening yet. I'd just decided to approach a couple on a yawl and see if I could get any more information when, over on the Customs Quay,

I saw a car arriving that I knew well—a very lush Sunbeam Talbot 90 in cream and sage. My pulse quickened. I'd been wondering all day whether I should see Mollie Bourne on this assignment, and here she was. I felt, among more disturbing emotions, a faint satisfaction that I'd beaten her to Falmouth. Mollie was never easy to get ahead of. In fact, she had a reputation in Fleet Street for being so far ahead of everyone else that on occasion she helped to make the news rather than report it—and that sort of reputation wasn't earned lightly.

I quickly gave up the idea of visiting the yawl, and rowed in towards the quay instead. Mollie had already got hold of a boat, and I intercepted her fifty yards from the shore.

"Hallo, Hugh," she said, and gave me a friendly-colleague sort of smile that must have taken a bit of practice. I thought again how breathtakingly lovely she was, with her rich chestnut hair and dark eyes and wonderfully creamy complexion. If I hadn't already fallen for her, I could easily have done so then. She was wearing a very simple summer dress that had probably cost the earth, and in spite of the warm evening she looked as cool as a shower. No one would have guessed she'd just driven nearly three hundred miles.

She made a little gesture towards the Attwood yacht. "What's happening?"

"Nothing," I said. "Everyone's being mum." I asked her if she'd heard about the shot secretary and was delighted to find that she hadn't. I gave her the few facts that I knew.

"Big stuff," she said coolly, but I wasn't deceived. There was a gleam of professional excitement in her eyes as she took in the covered windows of the yacht, the police guard, the floating reporters. She must have decided that the situation was in hand, for she suddenly relaxed.

"Well, it's nice to see you again," she said, in a carefully detached voice. I doubted if she'd forgotten a certain fairly passionate session we'd had together a few months earlier, but the memory certainly didn't obtrude. "You're quite a stranger."

"That's hardly my fault," I said wryly. Actually, I'd made at least half a dozen attempts to date her up since those incredible three days in May when we'd nearly come to grief together on the Loddon Castle story, but I'd only managed to see her twice and I hadn't made any further headway with her. "How *is* the *Courier's* spoiled darling?"

"Busy," she said.

"And elusive."

"Well, you know I'm wedded to my job."

"It's an unhallowed union."

"I don't think so."

"What's more," I said, "there's no future in it."

She laughed. "There's quite a good present."

"If you mean lots of lucre, yes," I said, with a pointed glance at the Sunbeam Talbot.

"I mean lots of interest," she said reprovingly. She turned her boat a little so that she could keep an eye on *Wanderer*. "I'd say this was going to be quite a story."

"I'm surprised you're not a guest on the yacht," I said.

She laughed again. "Actually, I *was* asked, but I had another engagement."

"I don't believe you," I said. "I think you're slipping."

"Do you? We'll see."

She dipped her oars and began to pull gently towards the yacht. I kept pace with her. As we moved in among the other boats a voice said, "Hallo, Curtis, you down here?" and I stopped to chat to a photographer I knew. The next thing I saw was that Mollie had rowed in close to the starboard side of *Wanderer* and was talking to a man in white trousers and a reefer jacket who'd emerged from the saloon. We converged on her instantly, like ducks rushing for bread. The man disappeared, and Mollie called out to us, "Mr. Attwood's going to see us all on board in five minutes."

If there'd been any sense of fair play in Fleet Street, she'd have been given a handicap!

Chapter Three

A few moments later the police came trooping out. They brushed aside all attempts to question them and left at once in their launch. Very soon the man in the reefer came to the rail again and said we could go aboard. There were so many rowing boats that we had to tie them all together and make a raft for the chaps on the outside to walk over. Then we filed up the gangway and crossed the beautifully laid deck to the saloon. Dusk was just beginning to fall, and someone switched on the lights as we entered. It was a small but very pleasant saloon, tastefully appointed in a modern style.

Bruce Attwood, an unmistakable figure to anyone who'd ever seen his picture, was sitting at the head of the table. He looked unbelievably like a stage tycoon. He was a big, florid man of sixty-five or so, with gleaming white hair, a commanding nose, and heavy jowls. He was obviously strained and tired after his long ordeal, but he still managed to convey an impressive air of authority.

He said, "I'm afraid there's only limited accommodation, gentlemen—you'll have to dispose yourselves as best you can." Then he noticed Mollie, and he half rose and drew out a chair for her. He waited until we'd draped ourselves round the walls and had our note-books out, and then he introduced the other people present. The man in the reefer was his guest, Basil Rankin. In addition, there was the captain, John Harris; his mate, Tom Quigley; a young steward named Bob Crisp; and a cook named Wilson.

"Well, now," Attwood said, "all of us in this ship have had a very exhausting time and we'd like to get to bed, so if you don't mind we'll keep the proceedings as short as we can. As I expect you know, we sailed from here last night, bound for the Riviera. Aboard were my guests, Mr. Rankin and his wife; my wife and myself; my secretary David Scott, and the crew of four. Just before one in the morning, when Harris was on the bridge and the rest of us were asleep, we encountered a small boat that appeared to be in trouble, and took two men aboard. They immediately produced guns, incapacitated the crew, shot my secretary dead, entered my wife's cabin, and made off with her jewel case."

He paused a moment, looking round. No one seemed at all surprised to hear about the jewels. Considering the way Charmian Attwood had flaunted them in public for years, an attempt on them had had to be made some time. The only really intriguing thing was that it had been made at sea.

"Right," he said. "Now I'll ask Harris to take up the story in detail."

I jotted down a note or two on Harris. He was a lean, brown, muscular-looking man in his middle thirties. White crowsfeet fanned from the corners of his blue eyes where the sun had failed to penetrate the creases. He had a wide, thin, rather bitter mouth. His face was drawn with fatigue, and he seemed to be feeling the strain even more than Attwood. There was, I saw, an ugly bruise over his left cheekbone. One way and another, he couldn't have looked grimmer if he'd just lost his ship through negligence.

"Well," he began, "we were about forty-five miles south of Falmouth, doing about twelve knots on a course to clear Ushant . . ." He spoke slowly and decisively, with a faint West Country burr that was attractive. "It was a pretty dark night, but clear, with a calm sea. I'd noticed a green light over to starboard and was keeping an eye on it as we passed about a couple of cables away, and then I suddenly saw a yellowish-white flare at the same spot. A flare at night is always reckoned to be a distress signal, so I changed course at once and went to investigate. The flare died down before I reached it, but the green light was still showing. I switched my searchlight on as I went alongside the boat, and saw that it was a small motor cruiser. Its engine was stopped, and it was drifting. A man called up that they'd had an explosion aboard and that his companion's arm was burned, and could they come up, so of course I said they could. I called up Quigley on the intercom and asked him to report to the bridge. Then I took the cruiser's rope and made her fast to us amidships and lowered the gangway. One of the men helped the other one up. Both their faces were black with smoke—or so I thought at the time—and the second one had an arm in a sling. They reached the deck just about the same time that Quigley arrived. I was just going to ring through to Mr. Attwood and tell him what had happened when both men suddenly pulled out guns and one of them said it was a hold-up and if we gave any trouble they'd shoot us. I thought maybe they were bluffing—anyway, I made a grab for the ship's siren to warn the others. But before I could reach it the man whose arm was supposed to be burned gave me a terrific wallop in the face and knocked me down, and then they stuck their guns into us and I didn't try anything else . . . The thing was, they sounded as though they meant business, and short of getting shot out of hand there didn't seem to be anything we could do . . ."

Attwood broke in, "Perhaps I should say at this point that in my view no blame attaches either to Harris or Quigley over the way they behaved. Men can't be expected to argue with guns—I wouldn't have tried it myself. Go on, Harris."

The captain's mouth had taken on a sardonic twist, and it struck me that he didn't attach a lot of value to Attwood's opinion, one way or the other. It was just a fleeting impression, but it stayed with me.

"Well," Harris went on, "they told us to go into the wheelhouse and sit down back to back and then one of them stuck gags in our mouths and lashed us together with a rope while the other one kept us covered. After that, one of them took something heavy from his pocket, I think it was a hammer, and smashed the radio transmitter. The other one went on deck and locked the door that leads to the forecastle, where Wilson and young Bob were asleep. Then they both went below. Quigley and I were doing our best to loosen the rope, but they'd done a pretty good job on us. There was a lot of noise coming from below—something that sounded like more hammering, and a scream, and some shots and shouting. But it didn't last long—the whole thing was over in three or four minutes. Then the two men came on deck again and disappeared down the gangway to their own boat. We were still struggling to get loose but it was another ten minutes before Quigley managed to wriggle out of the rope the rope and set me free. Then we both rushed below. We found that the doors of the cabins occupied by Mr. Attwood and Mr. Scott and Mr. and Mrs. Rankin had all been jammed from the outside with iron wedges driven in close to the latches. Mrs. Attwood's door had been locked from the outside, and the key left in the lock. I sent Quigley forward to get some tools, and I released Mrs. Attwood, and then Quigley and I got the other doors open after a bit of a struggle and everyone came out—except Mr. Scott. We found him lying dead on the floor of his cabin—one of the men had fired through his door from the corridor, and shot him. After a bit we went up on deck again, and there was no sign of the cruiser, and Mr. Attwood said we'd better put back to Falmouth, so we did."

Harris sat back, and dabbed his forehead with the sleeve of his uniform jacket. He looked grey, and just about all-in. The reporters got down his last few words, and waited, tense with interest. It was certainly a terrific story.

"Well, now, are there any questions you'd like to put to Harris before I go on?" Attwood asked. He was as methodical as a chairman at a board meeting.

There were a lot of questions. The first one, obviously, was whether Harris could describe the men—but he couldn't, not helpfully. Their faces, he said, had been completely blackened. Both of them had worn dark overalls and black berets, so there'd been nothing distinctive about them. Both of them seemed about average size. Harris thought they'd both been cleans-shaven, though he couldn't be certain about that because of the black on their faces. He didn't think there was a chance that he'd recognise either of them again if he saw them. Only one of them had spoken—the one who'd asked for help in the first place—and he hadn't said very much. He'd had a rough, growling sort of voice. Someone asked if it had sounded like a natural voice, and Harris thought not.

We asked him if he could describe the cruiser, and he was able to give us a pretty detailed account of that, because he'd had the searchlight on it. He said it had been about thirty feet long, or maybe a bit less, with a dark-painted hull, a short mast with a furled steadying sail, and an open cockpit aft. He hadn't noticed its name, and he hadn't got around to asking—he'd been too concerned with getting the supposedly injured man aboard. Some technically-minded reporter asked him whether the engine had sounded like a petrol or a diesel one and Harris said that no one aboard *Wanderer* had heard the engine and that the men must have made off under sail when the raid was over—perhaps because they didn't want the engine heard. It seemed rather odd, but that was all he could think of. Someone else asked what rope had been used for the lashing up, and Harris said there'd been a coil lying in a corner of the wheel-house and they'd used that.

As the questions died down, Attwood said, "Well, now, Quigley, can we have your story? Keep it short." He was evidently determined to tie the whole thing up for us in one sitting.

Quigley was a well-built young man of twenty-five or so with a head of very blond hair, an open, almost cherubic face, and a lot of freckles. He looked tired, too, but nothing like as tired as Harris. He said he'd been asleep in his cabin in the forecastle, and had been wakened by the sound of the engines going astern as Harris had come alongside the cruiser. He'd heard a voice hailing the bridge, but he hadn't been able to see anything because his cabin was on the wrong side of the ship. Then Harris had rung down, and he'd hurried on deck. He'd only had a brief glimpse of the cruiser, because the two men had pulled their guns almost at once, but Harris's description was about right, he thought. He said he wouldn't recognise the raiders if he saw them again, either. As far as the rest of his story was concerned, his impressions tallied exactly with Harris's. He'd heard the hammering and the screams and a couple of quick bursts from a gun, but nothing that everyone else hadn't heard.

"Well, now we come to what happened below," Attwood said. "I'm afraid my wife is too upset to talk to you herself at the moment—she and Mrs. Rankin have both retired to rest—so I'll have to give you the facts for her. She was wakened, as we all were, by a tremendous banging in the corridor outside the cabins. Before she could even get out of bed a man burst into her cabin, which wasn't locked, pointing a gun and a torch at her. She screamed, and called for me. The man went straight to her dressing-table and snatched up her jewel case. She heard some shots, and then the man rushed out, locking the cabin door behind him. His face was completely blackened and my wife, like the crew, doesn't think she would recognise him again. It was all over in a second or two, and he didn't say a word."

Attwood paused. "I, of course, didn't see him at all. I woke when the racket started and tried to get out of my door, but I couldn't. I heard my wife scream, and call out. I tried to batter the door down with a chair, but I only succeeded in breaking the chair. I tried to ring the bridge, but I couldn't get a reply. It was a pretty ghastly ten minutes, for me and for all of us, particularly after the shots. Finally, Quigley got my door open and I went out and we found poor David Scott lying dead."

Attwood looked at Rankin. "Anything to add, Basil?"

Rankin shook his head. He was a dapper little man of about fifty, with neat, greying hair and a grey toothbrush moustache. "Only that I tried to break out, too, but the door was too tough."

Attwood nodded. "Well, ladies and gentlemen, there's your story, and a very shocking one it is. Any more questions?"

Mollie said, "Could you tell us a little about Mr. Scott?"

"I'm glad you asked me that," Attwood said, "because it gives me an opportunity to pay tribute to him. He was a fine young fellow, a good friend of mine as well as a loyal servant, and his death is a great tragedy . . . If you want facts, he was thirty-five years old—Winchester and Cambridge, rowing blue, served in the Marines during the war with courage and distinction—just the sort of young fellow we can't afford to lose. He'd been my confidential secretary and close companion since 1951 . . . I can only add that

I shall leave no stone unturned to see that his murderes are brought to justice."

Someone said, "What have the police done so far, Mr. Attwood?"

"I'd say they've done a great deal in a remarkably short time—I've nothing but praise for them. Directly they learned what had happened they got in touch with the Admiralty police and the R.A.F. Search and Rescue Centre at Plymouth and a search was started for the cruiser right away. There was a big sweep by aircraft this morning, and the hunt has been going on all day. Of course, we've no idea where the boat went to after the raid, but there's been a general warning to shipping to look out for her. According to Harris, a fairly large cargo boat passed us on a westerly course shortly before the attack, and the authorities are trying to establish its identity and see if it can give any information. Beyond that the police have been busy all day with their routine inquiries, as you can imagine—photographing and measuring and taking statements. We've scarcely had a moment to breathe."

A reporter named Timmins, from one of the picture papers, said, "Can you give us any idea, Mr. Attwood, of the value of the jewellery that was stolen?"

"I can tell you it was very considerable," Attwood said.

"Could it be in the—well, the five-figure bracket?" Timmins pressed him.

He didn't have to press very hard. "It could be in the six-figure bracket," Attwood said grimly.

"Insured, of course?"

"Naturally."

There were a few more minor questions. We gathered that Bob Crisp, the young steward, and Wilson, the cook, had played no part in the affair at all until the very end, because the raiders had locked the door leading to the forecastle from below, as well as from the deck, and they'd both been confined in their quarters until Quigley had gone forward to get his tools and had let them out. The gags that had been used on Harris and Quigley, presumably to prevent them raising the alarm before the raiders reached the cabins, had been bits of torn-up sheet, which the police had taken away with them. The raiders didn't appear to have left anything else behind. We were all anxious to have a look round below, particularly the photographers, but Attwood said he couldn't have the ladies disturbed at the moment. If we cared to row out again in the morning, he'd be only too glad for us to take pictures and see anything we wanted to see. Asked about his plans, he said he thought they'd all be staying on board until after the inquest on David Scott, and beyond that they hadn't decided anything.

Someone thanked him for the way he'd organised the interviews for us, and he said he was always glad to help the Press and only wished it had been a less tragic occasion. Then we stampeded for the boats. It was quite dark by now, and even after Harris had switched the searchlight on there was a good deal of confusion and one reporter finished up in the water. I looked around to see if Mollie needed any help, but I needn't have worried—young Quigley, I saw, was handing her into her dinghy.

Ashore, there was another rush, this time for telephones. I was too late for a box by the quay, and had to drive several hundred yards before I found an empty one. There were scores of unanswered questions in my mind, but I hadn't time to consider them now. It was touch-and-go whether the story would make the early editions in any case—and I had more than enough material to be going on with. I got through to the office quickly and dictated my piece from my notes. It was a pretty rough job, but the subs. would knock it into shape and at this late hour the facts were all that mattered. Afterwards I was put through to the News Desk, and Blair answered the phone. By rights, he should have gone home hours ago, but he could never tear himself away if there was anything big happening. I gave him the gist of what I'd put over and he grunted happily, which was one of his ways of showing enthusiasm, and said it looked as though I'd need some help and he'd send Lawson down on the night train to lend a hand.

It was too late to make any more inquiries that night, and I set to work to find a bed. I had quite a job, what with the holiday-makers and the Press, but I finally got a room in a modest little pub called the Anchor, overlooking the square. I felt pretty tired myself after the all-day drive and the hectic evening, but my mind was active and I lay awake for some time, thinking about the raid. Technically, it had been a staggering achievement—it must have been planned to the last detail, and carried out by men with ice-cool heads. Men, I thought, who must have had an intimate knowledge of *Wanderer* and her movements—that would be a line to follow up. What I couldn't understand, what didn't appear ice-cool at all, was why they should have shot down David Scott, who'd apparently been safely shut up in his cabin like all the others and not in a position to do them any harm. It seemed, on the face of it, a singularly pointless bit of butchery.

Chapter Four

I breakfasted early, off coffee and rashers and all the newspapers I could lay my hands on. The sensational story had knocked almost everything else off the front pages, and the headlines—on the pattern of the *Record's* "Pirates Raid Attwood Yacht"—"Secretary Shot Dead" "£100,000 Jewel Haul"—were big and bold. But at this early stage the reports lacked variety, and I soon put them aside and began to think about the next moves.

I'd barely finished breakfast when Lawson arrived, full of enthusiasm for the story, and with a stack of papers as big as my own. He'd slept on the train and was very chipper.

"I see Mollie Bourne's down here," he said with a grin, after we'd exchanged greetings. "I hope you'll be able to-concentrate on the job, old boy."

I said I'd try.

"That's the spirit—keep a firm hand on your ugly passions and you should go far. Very dull road, though!" He picked up the *Record* and held it out at arm's length, gazing at the front page as reverently as though it had been an Old Master. "To think the customer gets all that for twopence!"

I smiled.

"Quite a hand-out old Attwood gave you, wasn't it?"

"Yes," I said, "he certainly got through the business."

"Anything you ought to fill me in on?"

I gave him my impressions of the people aboard *Wanderer* whom I'd met and told him a few minor details that I'd left out of my report. Then we got down to discussing the case. I mentioned the point about the raiders' obvious familiarity with *Wanderer* and

Lawson agreed it was a line to pursue. I also raised the point about Scott which had been bothering me overnight. "He wasn't in their way," I said, "so why should they have bumped him off?"

Lawson looked knowing. It was one of his most characteristic facial expressions. "As a matter of fact," he said, "the same thought occurred to me when I read your piece last night—and I've got a notion about it." He took a newspaper clipping from his pocket—a library clipping—and passed it to me. There was a strict rule against abstracting clippings from the library files, but Lawson never bothered much about rules. "Have a look at that," he said.

I had a look at it. It was a gossip paragraph from a London evening paper of September 1954. It was headed "Bodyguard", and it referred to an Attwood incident that had been reported a few months earlier. Apparently *Wanderer* had put into a North African port during a summer cruise when a nationalist demonstration had been in progress, and Attwood and his wife had been involved in what the paper called an "ugly scene" as they went ashore. In future, according to the paragraph, David Scott would accompany his employer on all trips in the capacity of bodyguard as well as confidential secretary. There were some personal details about Scott, which gave the impression that he was a pretty rugged physical specimen. The face in the accompanying picture was rugged, too, in a good-looking way.

I passed the clipping back. "Bodyguard or not," I said, "he was still shut up in his cabin."

"I dare say, old boy, but bodyguards often carry guns. It's just a thought, but maybe Scott had a gun. If so, he wouldn't have been at all inoffensive."

"If he did have a gun," I said, "he didn't use it—at least, I don't think so. If any of the shooting had been done by him, outwards through the door, there'd have been marks on the other side of the corridor, and nobody mentioned any."

"Maybe he didn't have time to shoot. The raiders might have known he had a gun, and shot him up before he could make a move."

"If so, they chose a pretty chancy way of doing it," I said, "jamming up his door and then shooting through it. Wouldn't it have been easier for them to open his door and shoot him before they started their operations?"

"Then he'd have had a chance to shoot them first ... I know this is all speculation, but I think it's worth looking into."

"Well, yes," I said.

"Right. Now what I propose, old boy, is that we tackle the police first and see what they've got that's new, and after that we'll have a browse around the yacht. I suggest you concentrate on this question of how the raiders knew so much about *Wanderer*, and I'll pick up what I can get, and we'll pool our ideas later. Okay?"

"Okay," I said. Since Lawson was senior to me, and also a Crime Reporter of great experience, I usually deferred to him on tactics when we were working on a story together.

The police station was only a short distance from the pub, so we walked. A dozen reporters were already there, standing about in groups. We gathered that Superintendent Anstey had promised to make an early statement, and soon after ten-thirty a constable came out and said he was ready for us and we all filed in.

Anstey was a big, heavy-chinned, formidable-looking man, but his manner to us was friendly. No doubt he realised that he needed us as much as we needed him, for the first thing he told us was that so far they'd had no luck in tracing the raiding cruiser in spite of a most intensive sea hunt. Apparently the aircraft which had gone out the previous day from the R.A.F. Search and Rescue Centre had been at the scene of the raid very soon after dawn, or about four hours after the incident had occurred. The raider, at that time, could hardly have been more than fifty miles away. They'd flown round and round in widening circles and in excellent visibility, but had seen no small cruiser within that radius. The conclusion seemed to be that the raider had been no longer at sea—that it must have put in, in fact, to some creek or harbour. The part of the coast that was considered to have been within its reach stretched roughly from the Fal in the east to Penzance in the west, a distance by sea of sixty or seventy miles, and took in the whole peninsula of the Lizard. Checking up on the many tiny harbours, Anstey said, would be comparatively easy—the real problem was the maze of quiet creeks on the eastern side of the peninsula. The great inlet of the Fal, running ten miles up to Truro, itself had innumerable branches that would all have to be searched. A few miles to the south of it, the Helford river presented an even more complex pattern of inlets. A large number of small naval craft were being used on the job, and a good deal of ground had already been covered, so far without result. A complicating factor was that the cruiser described by Harris was by no means an unusual type of boat, and among the many hundreds of holiday craft in local waters there were certain to be quite a number sufficiently like her to require investigation. Publicity by the Press might well shorten the search, and Anstey said he'd be grateful for our full co-operation. That, of course, was very satisfactory for us, too. It meant that from now on we were going to have a smooth passage as far as the police were concerned.

After that, he gave us some general facts. Scott, he said, had been shot in the side of the head, above the left ear, and must have died instantly. Altogether, six shots had been fired through the door, all in slightly different directions. Four of the bullets had embedded themselves in the cabin wall opposite the door and one, untraced, was presumed to have gone out through the open port. A local man raised the point about why he should have been shot at all, and Anstey admitted he couldn't offer any satisfactory explanation at that stage. Someone asked him if there'd been anything about the state of Scott's door to suggest that the secretary might have been on the point of breaking out, but Anstey said no, the door and the latch had been quite intact. He showed us the wedges that had been used to jam the doors—small, carefully-shaped slivers of iron, chisel-sharp at one end. They'd probably been cut, he said, from bits of old scrap, and he doubted if they'd be much use as clues. They'd been checked for fingerprints, but had been handled by too many people before the police arrived to be of any help in that respect. The gags had been carefully examined, but they might have been torn from any one of a million household sheets. A full description of the stolen jewels had been circulated in the usual way, though it was hardly likely the raiders would try to dispose of them while they were still hot. The jewel case, Anstey said, in answer to a question, was of small attaché-case size, with a lizard skin finish.

I left it to Lawson to raise the question of Scott having a gun. He didn't mention it in front of the others, but button-holed Anstey afterwards. The superintendent read the newspaper clipping and listened carefully to Lawson's ideas. Then he slowly shook his head.

"There was no gun in Scott's cabin, or among his effects," he said. "We made a routine check on all his things, and we'd certainly have found it."

"I see," Lawson said. "All the same, Superintendent, if the raiders knew about this bodyguard stuff they might have *thought* he had a gun, mightn't they? They could still have shot him up as a precaution."

"That's possible," Anstey agreed.

Lawson looked pleased. At least he'd got a good talking point for his story.

We left the station and walked across to the harbour. The weather was still wonderfully fine, and there seemed to be even more boats in the anchorage than there had been the previous day. The newspaper stories had brought a fresh wave of sightseers to the Prince of Wales Pier, and the pleasure boats were doing good business making a discreet circuit of Attwood's yacht before setting off for Truro and St. Mawes and the Helfore river. The Customs Quay was again comparatively quiet. There wasn't much water in the basin, but I managed to drag my dinghy out with Lawson's help and we rowed over to *Wanderer* and tied up to the raft of boats. The police had evidently finished their work aboard her, for there was no guard. Most of the reporters had already arrived, and Attwood appeared to be holding a sort of Open Day. Quite apart from his odd propensity for treating all newspapermen as his friends, he too, of course, needed our help badly. He was in the saloon with his dapper friend Rankin, deep in conversation with two men from the *Sentinel*. Charmian Attwood and Mrs. Rankin had come up for air, and were sitting under an awning on the after-deck, with a bevy of reporters round them. We were just in time to hear the story of the cabin raid all over again, and get Charmian's personal reactions. Strain and fatigue had taken some of the bloom off her, but I could still see she was a beauty. She had lovely facial bones, and glossy waving black hair and the most gorgeous big grey eyes. It was easy to understand why Attwood doted on her. By contrast, Rankin's wife looked insipid. She was pretty in a mousey sort of way, and very well-groomed, but she had a small thin mouth that I didn't care for. As a personality, she was completely eclipsed by Charmian, who of course was getting most of the attention and whose famous vitality kept breaking through in spite of her obvious depression over the tragedy.

Actually, there wasn't much to be picked up there except the fragrant scent of Chanel Number Five and presently Lawson nudged me and suggested we should go and talk to Attwood, who by now was free. Lawson produced his newspaper clipping again and asked Attwood if Scott had ever had a gun and if so whether the fact had been known by many people. Attwood was interested, and said Scott *had* had a gun a year or two back, though he certainly hadn't paraded the fact. He didn't know what had happened to it—probably Scott had just stopped taking it around as there hadn't really been any need of it. Still, in the absence of any better explanation of the shooting, he seemed to think Lawson might have got on to something with his theory of a precaution. We were still discussing the matter when more reporters arrived, and then we quickly dropped the subject and drifted away.

I couldn't see anything of Harris, but Quigley was showing small parties over the cabins and presently we joined one of them and went below. Quigley had quite recovered from the effects of the raid, and with his cheerful, willing manner he made the perfect guide. First, on the port side, came Attwood's stateroom, with a cracked door panel where he'd swung the chair against it. Next came his wife's, almost identical. We were allowed to stick our heads in, and Quigley pointed out, with a slightly cynical grin, the place where a hundred thousand pounds worth of jewels had rested on the dressing-table. Beyond, the Rankins had their double cabin.

Opposite them, on the starboard side, was another double cabin which hadn't been occupied; then a luxuriously-fitted bathroom; and finally Scott's cabin, directly facing Attwood's. It had been carefully cleaned up that morning, but there were still faint stains of blood on the floor that Quigley said he hadn't been able to get out. We examined the six bullet holes in the upper panel of the door, but they didn't tell us anything that we didn't know already. The panel was fairly thin but the door itself—like all of them—was very substantial and, as Anstey had said, showed no sign whatever of having been on the point of giving way.

We inspected the marks of the wedges in the three doors and Quigley showed us how they'd worked. They'd been driven in between the doors and the frames, just above the handles, with the result that the latches had been forced hard against their metal sockets, and though the doors all opened inwards it had been impossible to turn the handles from the inside. It was all very simple, but not something that could have been thought up by anyone unfamiliar with the doors. Quigley thought that driving in each wedge would only have needed one strong, well-directed blow, so that the three doors could easily have been jammed by two men before any of the occupants could reach the corridor.

I left Lawson talking to Quigley, and went back on deck to look for Captain Harris. This time I spotted him at once—he'd been buttonholed by Mollie up in the bows and she appeared to be doing quite a line with him. I didn't want to give her the impression I was trying to muscle in on her inquiries, so I hung back for a bit. Presently I saw her smile and nod good-bye to him, and as she departed along the other side of the ship I moved in. Harris was gazing out over the rail—he looked, I thought, like a man who'd be very thankful when he could put to sea again. As I approached he took a cigarette packet from his pocket, glanced inside it, tossed it overboard with an irritable gesture, and began to feel around for another pack. It seemed a good opportunity to start off on the right foot with him. I said, "Have one of mine, Mr. Harris."

He hesitated, then said "Thanks", and took one. I told him who I was, and said I imagined he must be getting pretty fed up with newspapermen by now. He looked a bit grim and said it certainly wasn't his line of country but he'd had instructions to give all the help he could, and that was that.

I said, "Well, there's one point I'd particularly like your view on. A thing that sticks out a mile in this buisness is that the raiders knew almost everything there was to know about *Wanderer*. They knew how to shut off the forecastle, they knew the best way of jamming the doors, they even knew the exact lay-out of the cabins. Not to mention that there was a length of rope lying handy in the wheelhouse."

He nodded at once—the approach obviously wasn't new to him. "I don't know that the rope's very important," he said, "there's usually rope lying around in a yacht. And of course up to a point it's easy enough for anyone who's interested to find out a good deal about a ship like this. There was an article about her in the *Yachting Journal* early in the summer, with specifications, plans of the lay-out, interior photographs with a good view of the cabin doors—almost everything . . . But not quite everything," he added.

"I don't suppose it said which cabin Mrs. Attwood occupied, did it?"

"I don't remember exactly, but I shouldn't think so—and it certainly couldn't have said which double cabin was going to be unoccupied on this trip. The raiders didn't even bother to jam that one."

"In fact," I said, "their information was right up to date."

"It looks like it."

"And surely there's another thing that points the same way," I said. "Could they have relied on intercepting the ship without knowing your course?"

"Relied?" He shook his head slowly. "I wouldn't say so. Mind you, it's been in the papers that we were going to the Med., and to get there from here you have to clear the Manacles and then set course to round Ushant. Anyone who could read a chart would know that. So they might have taken a chance . . ." He broke off. "All the same, it's not very likely. Some boats might pass close to Ushant, some might stand well off. And forty miles out from here, the difference in position would be quite a bit . . . No, I reckon you're right—I think they must have had a pretty good idea of our course."

"And wouldn't they have needed to know your sailing time and speed, too," I said, "to make an interception likely?"

He pondered. "Well, if they'd known we were planning to sail some time that evening, I suppose they could have hung about on the course until we showed up—but they'd have had to be pretty sure about their drift and leeway and the chances are they'd scarcely have known where they were after a while . . ." He shook his head again. "I certainly wouldn't have banked on an interception that way if I'd been them."

"Do you think there's any possibility they could have followed you out of here, and passed you, and taken up position ahead?"

"If they'd done that, I'd have seen them."

"Suppose they doused their lights?"

"It was still daylight when we sailed. They'd have had to wait for an hour or more before it was really dark—and by then they wouldn't have had a hope of catching us. That cruiser may have been fast, in fact she must have been to cover the ground she did, but she hadn't the lines of a speedboat—and we were doing twelve knots ourselves, don't forget . . . Still, if you feel like checking on sailings there'd be no harm in having a word with the coastguard look-out. He'll know."

"Where will I find him?"

"Up on the hill above St. Mawes."

"I think I'd better see him," I said, and made a mental note. "What it really boils down to, then, is that in your view the raiders must have had some up-to-date information about the ship, like the disposition of the cabins, and, in all probability, knew the course and speed and sailing time as well?"

Harris hesitated, but only for a second. "That's about the size of it—though it absolutely beats me how they could have done."

I said, "When was *Wanderer's* course and sailing time fixed?"

"Well, that's just it—it wasn't fixed till quite late. Sailing time was decided on when Mr. and Mrs. Rankin arrived—that was about teatime. Mr. Attwood had a talk with me, the way he always does, and said what about sailing at nine o'clock, and I said that was all right. Then about six I went up into the wheelhouse and laid off the course on the chart, jotted down a note about sailing time and speed, made the usual calculations about tidal drift and leeway, and worked out the course to steer."

"I suppose anyone on board could have seen these workings-out—the chart, the notes, and so on?"

"Well, yes ... I don't suppose Bob Crisp did, he was too busy, and so was Wilson, but there was no rule against it. The ladies weren't very interested, but Quigley knew, of course, and Mr. Scott—he always followed everything very closely—and Mr. Attwood had a couple of guests aboard that he and Mr. Rankin took up to the wheelhouse around seven ..."

"Extra guests, you mean?"

"Yes, he had a couple of chaps in for a drink—friends of his off a yacht called *Spindrift* that happened to be lying here."

"I see." I looked round the anchorage. "Can you point her out?"

"She's not here now—she sailed that same evening, an hour before we did. They said they were going to spend some time at St. Mawes." He gave me a twisted smile. "They didn't exactly look like pirates."

"Who does?" I said.

"Oh, I've seen plenty of chaps that did!"

I laughed. "What about strangers slipping aboard—intruders? Any possibility of that?"

"Not with all of us here—not a chance."

"Well," I said, "the information got around somehow, didn't it? Maybe someone had a last drink ashore before *Wanderer* sailed and spilled the beans without realising it. Do you happen to remember if anyone went ashore?"

"The two visitors did—they went in their own dinghy. They had some business in the town before they sailed."

"Anyone else?"

"No, I don't think so ..." He broke off. "Wait a minute, though—Mr. Scott went off just before eight to post a letter."

"*Did* he?" I said thoughtfully

Chapter Five

There didn't seem to be much more. I could usefully ask Harris at the moment, so I thanked him and went in search of Lawson. I found him by the port deck rail, deep in conversation with young Bob Crisp. I interrupted him to say I was going off on a couple of small jobs that would probably take me till lunchtime, and asked him if he could get someone else to ferry him ashore. He said, "Okay, old boy," with a slightly preoccupied nod, and I went on down the gangway to my dinghy.

As I rowed past *Wanderer's* stern, still pondering about the way that vital last-minute tip-off had been conveyed to the raiders, a new possibility suddenly occurred to me. The ketch *Morna*, which had been tied up only a few yards from *Wanderer*, was no longer there, and as I regarded the empty space it struck me that her owner would have been uniquely placed to receive information from anyone aboard Attwood's yacht. The two ships had certainly been within quiet-talking range, and a short message could easily have been passed by word of mouth from the stern of one to the bows of the other without attracting any attention. *Morna* herself, of course, didn't answer in the least to the description of the raiding cruiser, and apart from proximity I'd no grounds at all for suspicion, but it still seemed worth while to try and find out a bit more about her. I rowed on to *Curlew* to see if they could tell me anything. The plump man was on his way to the shore with a load of ship's rubbish for the waste basket, but John Thornton was in the cockpit, stripped to the waist and peeling potatoes. He greeted me with a grin and said, "So I didn't get my name in the paper after all?" I explained that there'd been a spate of information after I'd left him, and he said he quite understood. He was keen to hear the latest developments in the *Wanderer* story, and I told him what I knew. Then I asked him about *Morna*. He said she belonged to an elderly man who was cruising with his wife and two boys, and that she'd sailed that morning around nine. He didn't know where to, but I'd already lost interest. The raid on *Wanderer* had certainly not been the work of a family man.

I continued on my way to the Quay, tied up the dinghy, and collected the Riley. I studied the map for a moment, and then set off for St. Mawes. By water it was only a mile away across the Carrick Roads, directly opposite Falmouth; by land it was the best part of twenty miles, with a ferry to cross. Still, I thought I might need the car when I got there, so I took the longer route. I got directions for the coastguard look-out before I reached St. Mawes itself, and drove straight up there. The man on duty confirmed what Harris had said—it seemed that the police themselves had raised the question whether *Wanderer* had been shadowed out to sea, so he had the answer off pat. No boat had left Falmouth waters on the night of *Wanderer's* departure in time to have any hope of catching her.

I thanked him, and went on down the hill, and parked the Riley by the harbour wall at St. Mawes. It was a picturesque little place, with colour-washed cottages lining blue water and several luxury hotels and a lot of well-to-do people messing about in boats with enormous enthusiasm. I quickly sought out the Harbour Master's office and asked a man there if he knew a yacht called *Spindrift* and if she was still around. He said she was, and pointed her out to me at once—a handsome white cutter, of fifteen tons or so, riding to her anchor a few hundred yards out in the estuary. She'd come in, he said, two nights before at about nine o'clock, and had been there ever since. I asked him if the occupants had come ashore on the evening of their arrival, and he said they had—they'd inquired about taking water aboard, and afterwards they'd gone into the Crown for a drink. I borrowed his glasses and had a look at the yacht, and saw that her dinghy was tied up alongside. Someone was evidently aboard.

I'd just left the office when there was a squeal of tyres and a familiar sage-and-cream car pulled up sharply beside the Riley. Mollie looked out and waved.

I walked across to her, trying not to appear in a hurry. "Hallo," I said. "Following me again, eh?"

"I'm doing nothing of the sort," she said indignantly. "Who talked to Harris first, anyway?"

"We obviously think along the same lines," I said. "It's an affinity. I always knew we were made for each other."

She gave me a charming smile.

I said, "I assume you're interested in *Spindrift*."

"Mildly."

"The way you're interested in me!" She ignored that.

"As a matter of fact," I said, "I was just thinking of going out to her. What about suspending hostilities for half an hour and making it a joint trip?"

"I suppose we might as well," she said, "Just for half an hour. But after that it'll be war to the knife again."

"Oh, I know the rules," I said.

We soon found a fisherman to take us out, and a few minutes later we were alongside *Spindrift*. The two men aboard her certainly didn't look in the least piratical. One was white-haired, rubicund, and sixtyish—he could have been a retired Army man. His upper lip was so stiff that his speech was barely articulate. The other, who turned out to be his son, had the accents of a B.B.C. announcer. We introduced ourselves and they asked us aboard, politely, but with no great warmth. They proved to be an impossible pair to pump. Their name was Erskine-White, they were on a holiday cruise, they had known Bruce Attwood for several years, and they thought the raid on *Wanderer* was a very bad show—and that, it appeared, was about as far as we could hope to get without forceps. Naturally what I really wanted to know was whether, on going ashore, one of them had got in touch with an accomplice and given him particulars of *Wanderer's* sailing time and course, but it was scarcely a question one could ask! I did explain how we'd come to the conclusion that the raiders must have had late knowledge of *Wanderer's* plans, and Mollie followed up by asking if either of them had happened to mention the matter to anyone at St. Mawes after their arrival. They said they hadn't, rather stiffly, and that virtually ended the interview.

"Cagey, weren't they?" I said as the little boat took us back to the quay.

"Or else just stuffy," Mollie said.

"I suppose we ought to try and find out whether they telephoned anyone while they were at the Crown? Or met anyone they seemed to know?"

"That's going to be a tricky inquiry," she said.

"I know. Perhaps it would be better if only one of us went."

She nodded. "Let's toss up. The loser can go."

I said, cautiously, "I take it war to the knife doesn't start again until after this interview?"

"Agreed!"

I spun a coin, and she lost. She was in the Crown so long that I began to wish I'd lost. I wondered what tarradiddle she was making up to explain her questions.

At last she emerged, looking rather thoughtful. "Well," she said, "apparently the younger one *did* ring someone up."

"Really!" I said. I'd scarcely expected it.

"Not that it gets us anywhere," she added. "He was probably ringing Mamma at Bournemouth!"

"It was a coin box, I suppose?"

She nodded. "He had to get change for it—that's how they knew."

"Anstey could probably get the call traced."

"M'm!" She didn't sound very enthusiastic. "I think I shall let it ride for a while—I don't believe they had anything to do with it. But you do as you like, of course."

I said, "What I'd like to do is take you to lunch, now we're here."

"No, I'd better get back," she said, "I've got a lot of loose ends to clear up. Thanks all the same."

"If the *Courier* didn't squander so much on you," I said, "they might be able to afford to send someone down to help you!"

"Do I seem to need help?" she said, and smiled. "Good luck, Hugh—see you later."

It was nearly half past one when I got back to Falmouth, and I went straight to the Anchor. Lawson was in the bar.

"Ah, there you are!" he said. "I was just wondering what had happened to you." The sea air had given his pallid face a touch of colour, and I thought I detected an undertone of excitement in his manner. He bought me a bitter, clutched my arm, and took me off conspiratorially into a corner. "Well, did you get anywhere?"

I told him about my talk with Harris and my trip to St. Mawes. He listened, but only, I thought, with half an ear.

"Well, now, old boy," he said as I finished, "I think I may be on to something."

"Really?"

"Yes, I've got a theory that might tie the whole thing up. Including why Scott was killed. Especially that."

"I'm all ears."

He dropped his voice. "You know what I always say—'*cherchez la femme*!'"

"I know you always practise it," I said. I couldn't begin to guess what he was talking about, but I had a notion he was about to embark on one of the wildly defamatory reconstructions for which he was notorious in the office—and I was right.

"To start with," he said, "nobody's been paying enough attention to Bob Crisp—except me. He's an intelligent lad, and he doesn't miss much. He came back with Quigley, remember, after Quigley had fetched the tools that night, and he was in the corridor when Harris and Quigley unjammed the doors, and he saw and heard everything that happened. And do you know what did happen?"

"I haven't a clue," I said.

"Then I'll tell you. When Scott's door was opened, and our Charmian saw him lying there in a pool of blood, she gave a cry and dropped down on her knees beside him and said, 'Oh, *David*!'"

"What would you expect her to say—'Oh, Jonathan!'"

"Be your age, old boy—according to young Crisp she was in a

frightful state. Trembling and crying—all that stuff. She was obviously very fond of him."

"He was probably quite a stout chap."

"That's not all, either. I've been putting in a lot of work this morning. I managed to get Sylvia Rankin on her own, and I steered the conversation round to this scene in the corridor and I made it pretty plain what was in my mind."

"I bet you did," I said.

"I thought she'd freeze me, but she didn't. Between you and me and the gatepost, old boy, I don't think she likes Charmian very much. It's the husbands that are pally, not the wives. Anyway, when I hinted that Charmian and David must have been on pretty good terms, she gave me a bitchy, meaning sort of look and said, 'Well, Mr. Lawson, David was a very charming man, and Mr. Attwood isn't as young as he was, is he?'"

"Delightful woman!" I said.

"Sure—but why should we complain?"

"Anyway, what's your theory?"

Lawson leaned forward earnestly. "Suppose Charmian and David Scott were having an affair—been having one for years. Suddenly Attwood finds out about it, the way people do. He's beside himself with jealousy and rage. He makes up his mind to get rid of the lover. But he daren't do it in any of the straightforward ways, because if the story of the affair leaks out he's got too much motive. So he thinks up a clever plan. What he does is, he hires a couple of tough characters who'll come and raid his ship and bump off Scott—in return for the jewels, don't you see? It's a good proposition from all their points of view—the raiders get a lot of lolly, and as the jewels are insured Attwood doesn't lose either. In fact, he's absolutely nothing to worry about. All he has to do is brief the chaps about *Wanderer's* lay-out, and then tip them off about her sailing time—which is easy, because he's the boss, he's the one who makes the decisions—and they look after everything else . . . Well, what do you think of it?"

"Let's phone it right away," I said.

"Don't be an ass, old boy—I'm serious. I don't mean I've thought it all out to the end, but what's wrong with it as a working theory?"

"Well, you haven't got anything very solid to back it up with, have you?" I said. "This idea of yours that Charmian and Scott were having an affair is the wildest speculation—and probably quite untrue. She'd naturally have been cut up if she'd known him a long time, and liked him, and suddenly found him lying dead on the floor. She didn't have to be his mistress to show a bit of feeling. And she certainly didn't behave like a bereaved mistress to-day—my impression was that she was bearing up pretty well."

"Yes, old boy, I dare say," Lawson said knowingly, "but don't forget she was once an actress. A model, anyway—it's all the same thing. She's got herself in hand now, that's all. In the corridor she was caught off guard and showed what she really felt. There's no smoke without fire, you know."

"Well, I'd need a lot more evidence," I said. "Besides, even if there was something between them there's no reason to suppose that Attwood found out. That's just speculation again. And if he did, I still can't see him in the role you've given him."

"Why not? We know he's crazy about his wife. We know he gets violent at the drop of a hat—remember that car incident when he took a poke at some inoffensive chap? Strong passions, powerful emotions—that's Attwood. And he's just the type to enjoy working out a complicated plan—it's the breath of life to these tycoons."

I shook my head. "I don't think he's the type to hire ruffians to do a job for him. I just can't see it. And anyway, why go to all that trouble to organise a fake piracy when Scott could easily have been waylaid and knocked on the head by the same blokes on land . . .?"

"That would have cost Attwood much more. No insured jewels."

"He could have arranged a fake burglary when Scott was staying at his home . . . Anyway, there's a vital point you've forgotten. You say Attwood could have tipped off the chaps about *Wanderer's* sailing time, but he couldn't have told them her course. It was Harris who laid off the course, and after that Attwood didn't go ashore."

"According to you," Lawson persisted, "Harris said the raiders could have taken a chance without knowing the course. Maybe they did."

"Well, I'm sorry," I said, "but I can't buy it. I couldn't be less convinced."

Lawson looked a bit sulky. "I suppose you've got a better theory?"

"As a matter of fact," I said, "I think I've got one that's just as good."

"Oh? Well, let's hear it."

I took a long drink, enjoying his impatience. "Scott was a crook," I said. "He wormed his way into Attwood's confidence because he was a crook. He wanted the jewels—a third share, anyway. He planned the raid with two other crooks. The accomplices were waiting around here the night *Wanderer* sailed. Scott knew about the course, sailing time, lay-out, everything. He went ashore, ostensibly to post a letter, and told them all they needed to know. They had their cruiser handy in some convenient creek and they dashed off to it and put to sea. They carried out the raid, and when they got aboard *Wanderer* they shot up Scott because they didn't want to have to split the loot three ways. How's that?"

Lawson stared at me. "Do you believe that?"

"No," I said, "but it's not impossible, is it?"

"Old boy," he said solemnly, "I'm surprised at you speaking ill of the dead!"

Chapter Six

It was well into the afternoon when we called at police headquarters again to see how the search for the missing cruiser was progressing. The visit was nicely timed, for it seemed that Superintendent Anstey had just received a final report from the naval authorities. He didn't look very happy about it, either. The naval launches, he said, had visited every creek in the Fal estuary and every creek in the Helford river; they'd checked with every harbour between Falmouth and Penzance; they'd patrolled the whole of the rugged Lizard coast to make sure the cruiser hadn't been tucked away among the rocks of some inaccessible cove. But they'd found nothing. Every boat remotely resembling the raider had been satisfactorily accounted for by its owner. Assuming that she'd started her trip from some part of the neighbouring coast, it was possible that inquiries would produce in the end someone who had knowledge of her, someone who remembered seeing her, but whether she was ultimately remembered or not the fact remained that she was not in the area now.

The only possible conclusion seemed to be that she'd managed after all to escape the notice of the Search and Rescue aircraft, and by now was far away—in France, or perhaps in Eire. The R.A.F. people, Anstey said, were reluctant to accept this—according to them their search had been so thorough and the weather conditions so good that it was almost inconceivable the cruiser could have been overlooked. But Anstey made it pretty clear that he himself accepted it. The scope of the search had been widened, he said, to take in Continental and Irish ports, and the French and Irish police were co-operating. The two men who'd carried out the raid might appear to have got away temporarily, but it was almost certain that their boat would be traced in the end, and then the trail would be taken up again.

That, of course, was Anstey's sop to the public. To us, the failure of the search came very much as an anticlimax. Indeed, it began to look as though the case would have little more to offer us, once we'd filed our stories for the day.

Then, in the early evening, there was a new and most intriguing development. Lloyds, it appeared, had succeeded in identifying the big cargo ship that Harris had reported seeing in the vicinity shortly before the raid took place. She was the *Northern Trader*, a British ship of about five thousand tons. Her captain, Frank Watts, had been radioed through the owners to see if he could give any information about the incident. He'd replied that both he and his second mate, who'd been on the bridge with him at the time, had seen the lights of a biggish motor yacht that had almost certainly been *Wanderer*, but that was all. They'd seen no other navigation lights, no searchlight, and no flare. If they'd seen a flare, Watts said, they'd have stopped to investigate.

It seemed an extraordinary turn of events. I could understand that the navigation lights of a very small cruiser might not have been visible from the bridge of a largish ship—that, after all, was why so many small boats were run down at night in the sea lanes. I could even understand that *Wanderer's* searchlight might not have been noticed if it had been directed straight down on to the cruiser on the side away from the cargo boat—as it would have been. But a flare at sea was another matter altogether; it would have been visible for miles, and could hardly have been mistaken for anything else. It seemed almost beyond belief that both the captain and mate of the *Northern Trader* would have failed to spot it.

I suggested to Lawson that we should go back to *Wanderer* and see what Harris had to say about the new development, and presently we rowed out there. The Attwoods and their guests were ashore, but Harris and Quigley were both aboard, and we told them what had happened. They were quite baffled, for the same reason that I had been. The searchlight, Harris said, had only been on for a short time, because at close quarters the men on the cruiser would have been dazzled by it, so that was understandable; and as for the cruiser's navigation lights, he and Quigley both agreed that they'd been rather dim as well as low in the water and could easily have been overlooked. But the flare, Harris said, should certainly have been seen. It had burned for a couple of minutes, with a yellowish sort of flame—the sort of flame you'd get by setting a light to paraffin-soaked rags. He wouldn't be drawn into saying anything for publication about the *Northern Trader's* skipper, but he made it pretty clear that he didn't think Captain Watts could have been keeping much of a look-out.

After that, Lawson and I returned to the pub to write our story. The material we had didn't add up to any coherent picture, but there was plenty of it. There was the description of the cabins, the facts about Scott's death, the mystery of why he had been shot at all, the interview with Charmian Attwood, the stuff I'd got about the difficulties of interception and the problem of how the raiders had procured their up-to-date information, the total disappearance of the cruiser, and now this latest puzzle about the *Northern Trader*. Some of it had to be handled cautiously, for fear of libel, but in the end we knocked it all into a workmanlike story and phoned it. Then we relaxed. At least, I did. Lawson looked as though he hadn't entirely discarded the theory he'd put forward earlier. Anyway, he seemed very preoccupied, and he turned in early.

I didn't see him at breakfast next morning. There was a note from him under my door saying he'd thought up a new angle and had gone off to make some inquiries and would see me at the inquest on Scott, which was timed for eleven. That gave me a leisurely hour with the papers. I read through our rivals' efforts with the usual slight sense of apprehension, in case someone had discovered some major fact that had escaped us, but to-day no one had produced anything sensational. Most of the stories emphasised the new mystery aspects of the case—how it was that the raider hadn't been found, or the flare seen. One paper had talked to the Search and Rescue people and got an emphatic statement scouting the idea that the cruiser had got to France. Another had arranged its own radio contact with the captain of the *Northern Trader*, though the results scarcely seemed to justify the expense—he'd merely repeated what Anstey had told us. As always, I read Mollie's story with special care. Her pieces invariably gave the impression of having been written with effortless skill, but there was nothing very distinguished about this one. She'd covered the facts, like everyone else, and that was all. However, she'd still need watching. Her technique, as I knew only too well from personal experience, was to go ambling along quietly with all the rest of us, and then suddenly hurl herself and all her reserves through a gap that no one else had spotted. It was when she got a hunch that she was dangerous.

At ten I went along to the inquest on Scott. There was quite a crowd, what with the reporters and the whole of *Wanderer's*, passengers and crew and such of the public as could squeeze into the small room. Lawson arrived late, but he wouldn't have missed anything if he hadn't come at all. It was a long-drawn-out affair, but it produced absolutely nothing new in the way of evidence, and the verdict of murder against a person or persons unknown left us precisely where we were.

If the inquest was dull, what Lawson had to say to me afterwards wasn't. He was visibly simmering again, and could hardly wait to get me back to the pub for a quiet talk.

"You know, old boy," he said, as we settled ourselves in the bar, "I'm beginning to think there's something very very odd about this business."

I agreed that almost everything was. "But what strikes you as specially odd right now?" I asked.

"Why, this raider we've heard so much about—it's a bit of a ghost ship, isn't it? First it can't be found where it ought to be found, and now we're told it wasn't seen where it should have been seen. No flare, no nothing." He bent closer to me. "Maybe it never existed!"

I stared at him incredulously. "But, my dear chap we *know* there was a raider. Harris and Quigley ..." I broke off. "Just what are you suggesting?"

"Suppose the raider was an invention?" Lawson said quietly. "Suppose it was Harris and Quigley who bumped Scott off for Attwood, and got the jewels in payment?"

I was speechless.

"That shakes you, old boy, doesn't it?—but it makes plenty of sense. This way, almost all the difficulties we've been up against just fade out. If the whole story of the raid was a fake, then there's no mystery about where the cruiser's got to, no mystery about why the flare wasn't seen, no problem of interception, no problem of knowing the arrangements aboard *Wanderer*. Harris and Quigley knew everything. They knew where the jewels were, they knew the lay-out of the cabins, they knew how to shut off the forecastle so that young Crisp and Wilson couldn't put a spoke in, they knew the best way to jam the cabin doors. And there was nothing to stop them making up the story of a raider, because no one else aboard was in a position to know whether there'd been one or not . . ."

"Go on," I said.

"Well, as I see it, this is what could have happened. The two of them had the wheelhouse to themselves. They blacked their faces, put on working overalls and berets that they'd got specially, knotted up a piece of rope so that it looked as though it could have been used for tying them, fixed up a couple of gags to be found later, and went down to the corridor with wedges they'd already made. As soon as they were down there they jammed up the doors. One of them went into Charmian's cabin and pinched the jewel case—*without speaking*, don't forget. If he'd spoken, it would have given his identity away, because she knew him—as it was, she hadn't a clue about him. The other one shot up Scott through the door according to plan. Then they chucked the gun and overalls and berets overboard, cleaned themselves up, went back to the wheelhouse, waited a bit, came down and let everyone out, and told their story about the raider. And there you are!"

"It's fantastic!" I said.

"Of course it is, but the whole affair's fantastic—and this way, at least things fit . . . Look, take that business of the cruiser *sailing* away, when if she existed at all she must have had a perfectly good engine. I ask you, is that likely? Obviously the chaps would have wanted to make their getaway as quickly as possible. I know the suggestion is that they didn't want their engine to be heard in case the sound of it gave something away—but that thought came from Harris, don't forget, and I reckon it's nonsense. It wasn't as though the ruddy engine would have played Rule Britannia or something!—no one would have remembered the note of an engine. Besides, with a description like Harris gave, what would the engine matter? Isn't it much more probable Harris *had* to say the raider had sailed away, because otherwise everyone aboard *Wanderer* would have expected to hear her engine—and no one had, because she didn't exist!"

I looked at Lawson with increased respect. This time he really had been doing some hard thinking. But objections came crowding into my mind so fast that I scarcely knew which one to raise first.

"What about Harris's bruised cheek?" I asked. "Someone must have hit him."

"Just corroborative detail, old boy. It wasn't much of a bruise—he could easily have got Quigley to dish it out. It would have been a small price to pay for all that dough."

"H'm! But, look, their behaviour afterwards was all wrong. If Harris and Quigley had been in on it, would Harris have agreed so readily that the raiders must have known all about the course and the sailing time and so on? Wouldn't he have tried to put us off that line?"

"How could he?—it stuck out a mile, as you said, and anyone could have given us the technical stuff. If he'd pretended you were wrong, and someone else had said you were right, that would merely have made us suspicious of him."

"At least he didn't have to volunteer the information that there was a cargo ship passing at the time."

"Didn't he? It would have looked pretty queer if he hadn't mentioned it, and the police had found out about it from the *Northern Trader* herself as they easily might have done. I reckon he had no choice."

I was silent for a moment. Then I said, "Well, there's another thing—if Harris and Quigley had been given the job of killing Scott, wouldn't they have wanted to make sure he was dead before they cleared off?"

"Perhaps they did. They could have unjammed his door and looked in and jammed it up again. Or perhaps they killed him first and jammed it afterwards. I tell you, old boy, everything's covered."

I slowly shook my head. "A lot of the details are covered, I agree—but not the principle. The whole thing's still based on your speculation that Scott was Charmian Attwood's lover which I doubt. And I still can't see Attwood as a man who'd employ crooks to do a murder for him. Leaving aside the question of whether he's capable of it, I just can't imagine him taking the risk. Think of the blackmail possibilities!—why, he'd have been putting himself in their hands for ever. He'd have been crazy."

"With a hundred thousand quid to share between them," Lawson said, "they wouldn't have had much need for blackmail. Anyway, they'd have been in his hands, too."

"But he'd have had a lot more to lose," I said. "Position, reputation, wife, wealth—a life he enjoys. He'd never have risked throwing all that away. It simply doesn't make sense."

Lawson lit a cigarette and pondered for a while. He was obviously reluctant to give up his theory, but he seemed less happy about it than he had been. Suddenly he said, "All right, old boy—I'm inclined to agree with you. Let's scrub out the business of Attwood and a lover for the time being. Maybe it was you who were on the right lines after all."

"What do you mean?" I said.

"Suppose Harris and Quigley and *Scott* were in it together. Three tough chaps on the make—you'll admit there's nothing fantastic about that. They knew about the jewels, and they decided to steal them by staging a fake raid. Then, at the last moment, Harris or Quigley shot Scott so that they wouldn't have to share the dough with him. Just as you said, in fact, except that Harris and Quigley are in it instead of two strangers. Now that really does cover everything."

"What did they do with the jewels?"

"They waited until they got back to Falmouth. Then one of them went ashore to ring the police—Quigley, wasn't it? He could have smuggled them into the tender and hidden them somewhere on land, temporarily. Or for that matter they could still be aboard *Wanderer*—I don't suppose anyone's thought of searching the ship. Why should they?"

I fell silent again. For the first time, Lawson really did seem to have produced a feasible reconstruction—up to a point. But I still boggled at the roles he'd cast his characters for, and I told him so.

"Take Harris," I said. "I agree he's a fairly tough egg—he probably wouldn't be a ship's captain if he wasn't. But if he's a murderer, I'm a Dutchman."

"Then I reckon you're a Dutchman," Lawson said. "I didn't tell you before, but I've been checking up on Harris—that's what I was doing this morning, before the inquest. I went to see him with a yarn about wanting to do a magazine piece—what it feels like to be a yacht captain for a rich man, that sort of thing. He wouldn't play, not for publication, but I did get some of his life story out of him. He's tough, all right—tougher than you think. He was in the Navy during the war, doing some of the cross-Channel commando stuff. You can bet he got pretty used to violence on that job. I can tell you something else—he's a man with ambitions. He started his working life in a boatyard, and he's got a passion for boats and everything that goes with them. What he really wants is to have a boatyard of his own. He said so. It's perfectly obvious he doesn't at all enjoy being pushed around by millionaires And a man with a tough streak will do a lot to get independence—even murder."

"Well, I still can't imagine Harris doing it," I said. "And what about Quigley? Now there's a likeable young chap, if ever I saw one. Can you see him as a murderer?"

"I can see almost anyone as a murderer," Lawson said, "if the stake's big enough . . ." The phone rang outside, and he waited to see if the call was for us, but it wasn't. "The trouble with you, old boy," he said, "is that you've got too much faith in human nature.

Quigley looks innocent enough, I agree, but he's probably under Harris's influence, and anyway that babyface stuff doesn't mean a thing. Never trust a face, old boy."

"Well," I said, "I'm not convinced—though I admit it's quite a theory you've got hold of . . . What are you going to do about it?"

"Somehow," Lawson said earnestly, "we've got to prove that the story of the raider was a fake. I'm absolutely certain it was, and there must be some way . . ."

He broke off, checked by a loud disturbance in the corridor. A chap named Ffoulkes, a *Morning Herald* man who was also staying at the Anchor, suddenly rushed past the open door of the bar as though a devil were after him.

"Something must have happened," I said, and went to the door. "What's the hurry, Bill?" I called out.

He was already in his car. He yelled back, "They've traced the boat that held up Attwood!" and roareed away.

I looked at Lawson. I must say, after the first second or two he took it pretty well. He even managed a rather sickly grin. He finished his drink with a deliberation that Drake would have envied, and said, "Well, even Homer rods, old boy. I suppose we'd better go and see what all this is about."

Chapter Seven

Word had got around pretty fast, and there were already a dozen reporters waiting at the police station when we got there. Not much had come out so far in the way of facts, but what had emerged had been sufficient to create an air of lively expectancy. It seemed that a man had called at headquarters and reported that his boat had disappeared, and from his description of it it had sounded very much like the raiding cruiser. He'd had a girl with him, and the two of them had been closeted with Anstey and his henchmen for nearly an hour and were still there.

We waited as patiently as we could, and just before three they came out. The man was tall, thirty-ish, curly-haired, and extremely good-looking in a bronzed, film star sort of way. The girl was a synthetic blonde in her twenties. Her face wasn't anything special but she had a most shapely figure, and she was got up to look an eyeful in the briefest of shorts and a tight cotton sweater. Both of them looked pretty browned off, and the man seemed rather dismayed to find so many reporters waiting. I think he'd have walked straight past us if we hadn't closed in and more or less blocked their passage.

There followed the kind of collective interview I've never much liked, with everyone firing questions at once in a disorderly way, but little by little we got the story sorted out. The man's name was Guy Mellor. He was, he told us, in an accent that matched the old school badge on his blazer pocket, a sales representative for a London firm called Cricklewoods who built marine engines. He owned a cabin cruiser called *Mary Ann*—a thirty-footer, with a dark blue hull, a small tanned sail, and an open cockpit aft. He'd brought her to Cornwall from the Solent, a fortnight previously, and had left her at a place called Gillan Creek, an inlet near the mouth of the Helford river. "You see," he said, with a slightly embarrassed glance at his companion, "we'd planned to do a fortnight's cruise to the Scilly Isles, starting to-day."

At that point Lawson caught my eye, gave a huge wink, and murmured out of the corner of his mouth, "Once aboard the lugger and the girl is mine!"

Someone asked if we might have the young lady's name. Mellor hesitated, but the girl replied promptly, "Gloria Drage."

Then Mellor took up the story again. They'd left London by car that morning at crack of dawn, hoping to get *Mary Ann* away well before midday, while there was still enough water in the creek to float her, and make Penzance before nightfall. But when they'd reached the creek they'd been dismayed to find that the boat wasn't there. They'd searched around for a bit but they hadn't been able to find any trace of her in the creek and in the end they'd come and reported their loss to the police. It was only then that Mellor had learned that his boat was similar to one the police were looking for in connection with the Attwood raid. Mellor had known next to nothing about the raid—he'd been in Belgium for a week on his firm's business and all he'd seen about the incident was a small paragraph in a French-language paper. When he'd got back to London, the previous afternoon, he'd been too busy packing for the holiday to spend time catching up on newspapers. Gloria said she'd read something about the raid, in the *Sketch*, but only some headlines, and she hadn't thought much about anything. She had an excruciatingly affected voice, with Cockney undertones.

There were a lot more questions we wanted to ask, but Mellor said they simply must get something to eat as they'd had no lunch, and after that they'd arranged to meet the police at a little place called Manaccan near Gillan Creek and show them where *Mary Ann* had been moored, so if there was anything else perhaps we could see him there. There'd be plenty of opportunity to talk, he added ruefully—it looked as though he might be around for some time! At that, Gloria's expression grew very sulky. We went with them to their car—a vintage and obviously treasured Bentley that was exactly what I'd have expected Mellor to have. It was crammed to capacity with kitbags, suitcases, gumboots, boxes of provisions, odd bits of boat's gear, and charts and guide books of the Scillies area. Gloria squeezed in, giving us an attractive display of brown thigh as she did so, and they drove off.

Lawson gazed after them with a look almost of compassion in his eye. "Now that's what I call real bad luck," he said. "The poor chap won't even be able to take a double room at a hotel, with all the publicity they're going to get . . . A recent pick-up, I'd say, wouldn't you? No engagement ring—and right out of his class. Probably a factory hand."

"You're a snob, Lawson," I said. "Anyway, has this anything to do with the story?"

"Not a thing, old boy—just a few reflections on the hazards of life! Let's go and see what Anstey has to say."

"Anstey was visibly relived that there'd been a positive development in the case at last. He said he'd no doubt at all that *Mary Ann* and the raiding cruiser were one and the same boat, and he hoped they'd find some useful clues at the creek. When he left for Manaccan half an hour later with a carload of his men, a long convoy of newspaper cars followed him. It was about fifteen miles from Falmouth to Manaccan, much of it by narrow and winding secondary roads, but with a police motor-cyclist riding ahead to warn holiday cars of our approach we got through without difficulty. The Bentley showed up at the tiny village soon after we arrived, followed almost at once by Bruce Attwood and Harris who'd been summoned from *Wanderer*, and presently Mellor led the whole party to the creek. The tide was low, and the river had dried right out, leaving no more than a trickle of water to mark the twisting channel. On either side of the channel stretched an expanse of flat mud, dotted with stones and patches of yellowish-black seaweed and a few lazy swans. The creek was about a hundred yards wide and was flanked by steep red-earth banks and tall conifers, with green fields sloping up behind them. A thin ribbon of road ran close beside the north shore, but the place where the cruiser had been left was hidden from the road by a screen of bushes. The exact spot was a tree-fringed bight, well off the fairway and very quiet. It was easy to understand now why none of the local cottagers had reported seeing a boat that answered to the raider's description, for the cruiser would only have been visible to someone walking down through the trees, and there was no path. It was equally understandable that no passing yachtsman had remembered and reported it, for Mellor explained that he'd left it anchored fore and aft with its bows pointing towards the fairway, and at that angle it would have looked much like any other boat. To get a good view, a yacht would have had to come right in, a pointless and possibly hazardous operation, since we gathered that even at high water the bight was pretty shallow.

Mellor pointed out *Mary Ann's* dinghy, which should have been drawn up under the bank and tied to a tree root, as he'd left it, but instead was sitting out in the mud, with its anchor down, in the spot where the cruiser ought to have been. Then the police got to work. They asked us to stand well back on dry ground while they investigated along the foreshore but they kept Attwood in formed of what was happening and we stuck with him. It wasn't long before they found quite a lot of interesting marks. In addition to a short keel mark at the edge of the mud where Mellor had drawn the dinghy out of the water, there was a second, longer mark where it had been dragged back in again. Mellor and Harris had a brief technical discussion with Anstey about tides, and everything seemed to fit. Mellor, it appeared, had left the dinghy late at night at the top of a high tide. If it had been moved in the evening of the day *Wanderer* had sailed, which was ten days later, the tide would have been appreciably lower so there'd have been farther to drag it.

Other things fitted too. Around the dinghy marks there were a lot of footmarks, and they hadn't all been made by Mellor's gumboots. Some were of other gumboots—two different pairs, Anstey thought. The picture was growing clearer. There was a little discussion about how the raiders could have got the dinghy out to the cruiser, since Mellor had hidden his own pair of oars deep in the undergrowth and they were still where he'd left them, but the view was that a good push-off and a little hand paddling would have been quite sufficient to take the dinghy to *Mary Ann* across the placid water of the bight.

We discussed, too, the question of how the raiders had reached the creek. It seemed pretty clear that they'd come by land, or they wouldn't have needed to use the dinghy. That suggested a car, since the creek was remote and they wouldn't have had much time to spare after learning of *Wanderer's* sailing plans. But if they had come by car—and there was no material evidence one way or the other, because the ground among the bushes was too hard to take any tracks—who had driven it away? Since it now seemed certain that the cruiser had escaped across the sea immediately after the raid, the likeliest answer appeared to be that there'd been a third person involved—someone who'd brought the raiders to the creek by car and driven it away afterwards. It was an intriguing new possibility.

Anstey's men were now busily taking photographs and making plaster casts of the footmarks. Attwood was talking to the superintendent. Some of the reporters had wandered off to see if they could pick up anything at the local cottages; some, the Sunday paper men, had left to phone their stories; some, including Lawson, had gathered round Mellor again. Nobody was paying much attention to Gloria, who was sitting by herself on a fallen tree trunk, looking very fed up. Presently I strolled over and joined her.

"Care for a cigarette?" I said.

She brightened a little. "Well, thanks—I don't mind if I do."

I lit it for her. "Rotten bad luck, losing your boat like this."

She nodded. "I don't know why he couldn't have had it looked after properly—it reely is too bad."

"Well—it ought to have been all right," I said. "It was a chance in a thousand."

"What I say is, when a girl only gets a fortnight's holiday a year and someone asks her to go away with him it's up to someone to see she's not let down."

I made a sympathetic sound.

"All that stuff he talked about blue sea and lovely islands and I don't know what—and now *this*!" She jerked her head petulantly towards the policemen. "It'll go on for days, too, I wouldn't be surprised. Fat lot of holiday we're going to get!"

"It may not . . ." I said. "Still, it must be very disappointing for you. Are you fond of sailing?"

"Me? I've never done any. I went on the Serpentine once, that's all."

"Well, perhaps you wouldn't have liked it. It's all right when the weather's like this, but it's a long way to the Scilly Isles and I believe it can be frightfully rough. Not much fun then if you're not used to it."

"Go on, you're just trying to cheer me up," she said. "Still, thanks all the same." She glanced across at Mellor, and suddenly got to her feet. "I'd better see what's happening," she said.

What was happening was that Mellor had been left alone with Mollie, who was talking to him in a very animated way. She didn't, I thought, appear to be getting a lot of response out of him, but she was certainly trying. Gloria gave her a pretty snooty look as she joined them, and Mollie detached herself. It seemed a good chance for me to have a few words with Mellor myself.

"Quite an Adonis, isn't he?" Mollie said, as she passed me.

"The blonde's not too bad," I said recklessly.

She just smiled.

Gloria had already moved on. I don't know what she'd said to Mellor, but whatever it was it hadn't cheered him up at all. I'd never seen anyone look more down in the mouth. As I strolled towards him, he turned and came to meet me, regarding me intently.

"I say . . ." he began, and broke off. "You are a reporter, aren't you?"

"From the *Record*," I said. "My name's Curtis."

He nodded, frowning. "Look, old chap, I wonder if you could give me a bit of advice. The fact is, I'm in rather a spot."

"Oh?"

"Why, yes—all this publicity. You see . . ." he threw a nervous glance in Gloria's direction ". . . well, the truth is, Miss Drage isn't exactly my girl friend—at least, she's not they only one. I—I thought she'd like to come on this trip, so I asked her, but it's going to be damned awkward for me if it gets around that I brought her." He gave a sheepish grin. "I'm going to lose one or two rather cherished telephone numbers! I suppose there isn't any chance of keeping her out of this, is there?"

I told him I didn't think there was a hope. "There must be forty or fifty newspapermen covering this story," I said, "and I don't know half of them myself. You'd never be able to round them up. Even if you did, they wouldn't all play ... Sorry, but I'm afraid you'll just have to face it."

He gave a rueful nod. "I rather thought that's how it would be. Ah, well, it's just one of those things, I suppose ... Pity I didn't leave the blasted boat in the Solent and go to Blackpool instead!"

"Had you had her long?" I said.

"Since March."

"Was she a nice boat?"

"Damned nice. I bought the hull cheap and had her converted and fitted out to my own ideas—did a hell of a lot of work on her myself, too, as a matter of fact. You have to, these days, otherwise it costs the earth. She looked fine when she was finished."

"Did she have a good engine?"

"First class. One of our own—reconditioned, but as good as new. At the price, there's no better bargain on the market." For a moment I thought he was going to try and sell me one. "She could do over ten knots, you know."

"Not bad," I said. "By the way, was she fuelled up for your trip to the Scillies?"

"Fuelled up, and all ready to put to sea. I reckon she had a range of a hundred and fifty miles with the spare cans I'd loaded. Those blighters wouldn't have had a thing to do, except take her away."

"I should think they must have known that," I said. "And that she was a sound boat. It would have been a frightful risk for them otherwise, wouldn't it?—setting off on a desperate raid like that with an unknown quantity on their hands. The engine might have conked, she might have sprung a leak—anything could have happened."

"I agree," Mellor said. "I suppose they must have reconnoitred her pretty thoroughly while she was lying here. It's quiet enough."

"It wouldn't have been an easy thing to do, all the same," I said, "not thoroughly. If I'd been planning a job like that, I'd have wanted more than a quick look—I'd have wanted a surveyor's report! I did wonder if you might have discussed her with somebody while you were down here and been pumped without realising it."

He regarded me thoughtfully for a moment, then shook his head. "No, I didn't discuss her with anyone—not round here. I was a bit pushed for time, so I just made her all shipshape and went off to Falmouth and got a train ... Of course, back in the Solent where I fitted her out, lots of people knew everything about her."

"Including that you were coming down here for a holiday in her?"

"Well, yes."

"Did anyone show a special interest?"

He considered. "Well, there was one chap who asked me if I'd sell her—he saw the engine go in, and thought she looked a nice job. He asked me a lot of questions about her, I remember."

"Who was he?"

"As a matter of fact, I haven't the slightest idea. I'd never seen him before, and I never saw him again. I think he was just looking over the yard. He was quite an old boy—reddish face, white hair."

I suddenly remembered the stuffy pair that Mollie and I had gone out to see aboard *Spindrif*. I said, "Had the chap a rather stiff manner, by any chance? Tall, clean-shaven ..."

"No, this fellow had a moustache. And rather a hearty manner, I'd say. Anyway, I don't see how he could possibly have been involved in this business—it was back in May that I saw him, long before I ever thought of going to the Scillies."

"When *did* you plan the trip?" I asked.

"Not till July—I didn't get my own holiday leave fixed till then."

I was just debating whether it was worth pursuing the subject of Mellor's Solent contacts any further when Gloria came up and joined us again, and I decided not to. "Well, let's hope you get the boat back, anyway," I said, preparing to push off.

"I certainly hope I do. It's damned worrying."

"Was she insured?"

"Yes, thank heaven!" He looked at Gloria. "The holiday wasn't, though, was it, Gloria?"

"No, and it makes me sick," she said.

"What do you think you'll do?" I asked Mellor. "Spend the fortnight here?"

He shrugged. "I suppose so—I doubt if I'll be able to tear myself away until I get some news. If the boat turned up, of course, we might still be able to make the trip ... Anyway, it's pretty good country here—I wouldn't mind doing a bit of walking myself."

"Catch me walking!" Gloria said.

"Well, there's always the car, Gloria—we can bat around in that. I'll think of something, anyway."

"You'd better," Gloria said. "*And* it had better be good!"

I left them to it. By and large, I didn't envy Mellor his girl friend.

Chapter Eight

Lawson and I stayed on at the creek for a little while longer, but it soon became clear that there weren't going to be any more developments that day. Attwood and Harris had already left, and presently Mellor and his girl went off to look for somewhere comfortable to stay in Falmouth The reporters had dispersed and the police were packing up. Soon after seven we returned to Falmouth ourselves and went into the Anchor bar to review the situation over a before-dinner sherry. There was no need to phone a story that evening, since it was Saturday and the *Record* wouldn't be appearing again till Monday morning.

Reviewing the situation didn't take long because there was so little now to go on. The identification of the raiding cruiser had not only wrecked Lawson's most ambitious and persuasive theory—it had thrown us right back into a thicket of insoluble problems. We still didn't know for certain what had happened to the cruiser; we still had no satisfactory explanation of why her flare hadn't been seen. Lawson made a half-hearted suggestion that perhaps the captain of the *Northern Trader* had been in too much of a hurry to stop and investigate, and having failed to stop had been obliged to say he hadn't seen it, but there was the second mate to consider, too, and one way and another the idea didn't seem worth pursuing. The point about the unnoticed navigation lights had been cleared up, after a fashion, but why the cruiser had sailed, rather tan motored away, was still a complete mystery. It wasn't as though there could have been anything wrong with an engine that in four hours had carried the boat outside the radius of the aircraft sweep. In addition, we were no nearer explaining how the raiders had managed to keep tabs on *Wanderer's* movements up to the last minute, or, convincingly, why David Scott had been shot. The whole case seemed wide open again.

Oddly enough, the only theory that now stood up at all was the one I'd thrown out jokingly as a counter to Lawson—that Scott had himself organised the raid with two other men, and tipped them off about *Wanderer* when he'd gone ashore to post his letter, and subsequently been shot for his share of the loot. But even that theory only covered some of the facts, and there wasn't really a shred of evidence for it. It certainly did nothing to clear up the latest puzzle—how the raiders could have dared to rely for their purpose on a stolen boat that might have let them down. Lawson scouted the Solent contact idea—he seemed to think it would have been altogether too much of a coincidence if they'd happened to find a boat that suited them, that happened to be about to make a trip to Cornwall, just at the time that Attwood's yacht happened to be sailing from Cornwall—and put that way it certainly didn't sound very likely. He thought it might be worth while telling Anstey about the man who'd tried to buy *Mary Ann*, in case Mellor hadn't mentioned it, but he didn't see that we could do much about it ourselves. On the whole, he favoured Mellor's explanation—that the raiders had made a careful reconnaissance of the boat in Gillan Creek. I said that at the very least they'd have had to run the engine, and Lawson said why shouldn't they have done—the creek would have been deserted enogh, particularly at night. I felt far from satisfied, but I couldn't suggest anything better.

We continued to chew over the case through most of the evening, but we made no appreciable progress. At ten-thirty, Lawson said, "Two minds without a single thought, that's us, old boy—let's call it a day," and we went to bed.

Sunday was, comparatively speaking, a day of rest. Indeed, one of the first things I saw from my bedroom window in the morning was Mollie emerging from her hotel opposite with a towel and a swimsuit and going off in her car for a swim. She was back in time to join the rest of us at the police station around ten, and we haunted the place all morning, though nobody expected much to happen. Mellor looked in about eleven to see if there was any news of his boat—Gloria, we gathered, had flatly refused to come with him. There wasn't any news, and he went off gloomily after a short talk with Anstey. Since there was so little doing, I took the opportunity to raise the question of *Spindrift's* movements with the superintendent, and tell him about the telephone call her occupants had made from St. Mawes. He was mildly interested, and said he'd see if he could get the call traced. As it turned out, he had no difficulty, because it had been a trunk call to Winchester. My first reaction was that that ruled out any possibility that it had been used to tip off someone about *Wanderer's* plans, but Lawson, more subtle, wouldn't have that. He said the people who'd been rung at Winchester could have been in on the conspiracy, and might immediately have phoned the information back to someone in Cornwall. Anstey agreed, and made further inquiries, and it turned out there hadn't been a single phone call from Winchester to the Falmouth area around that time. Of course, in theory a message could have been passed on from place to place several times before it finally came back to Falmouth, but there was no means of checking that. On the whole, I was inclined to think that *Spindrift* could be written off as a suspect.

The only other thing of interest that morning was that Anstey—with Mellor's rather rueful co-operation, we gathered—asked Scotland Yard to send someone along to have a look at Mellor's passport at his lodgings in twon and confirm that he really had been in Belgium! It was just a routine check, of course, and when the report came through it simply said that Mellor had been in Belgium and that the dates tallied with what he'd told us.

In the afternoon I went over the story again with Lawson and we discussed what we should send that evening. Quite a lot had happened since our last message—the inquest on Scott, the arrival of Mellor, the identification of the raider and the confirmatory discoveries at the creek—but the trouble was that all of it had been very adequately covered in the Sunday papers, and by Monday morning it would cut no ice at all. The best we could do was what

Lawson called a "think-piece"—a sort of round-up of the unanswered questions. The way things were going, it was beginning to look as though the story would soon die of undernourishment. Blair seemed to have the same feeling when I phoned our piece that evening. He hummed and hawed and fussed, and said it was all very disappointing after such a fine start, and weren't there any new angles, and in the end he said Lawson had better leave me to it and go back to town, because there'd been a razor slashing in Mayfair that offered more scope for him. Lawson was very peeved, especially when he learned that he was expected to catch a train at eight-fifty that evening that wouldn't get him to London until daybreak. However, Blair didn't sound in the mood to be argued with, and at eight-fifty I took Lawson to the train. His last words to me, with a characteristically lecherous grin, were, "I don't have to remind you to keep an eye on Mollie, do I?" and I said he didn't.

I felt a bit flat after Lawson had gone, and presently I walked across the square to Mollie's hotel, the Falcon, to see if she was around, but she wasn't. Then I thought I'd see what Mellor was doing, because his hotel was next door, and I went into the bar there. I found him—and Mollie, too! They were sitting in a corner together. He was drinking beer and Mollie was drinking whisky—a thing I'd never known her to do before. She was looking very gay, and seemed to be doing most of the talking. Mellor, I thought, looked a bit hemmed in. There was no sign of Gloria.

I walked over to them and said "Hallo!" Mellor said, "Why, hallo, there!" in a friendly way, and beckoned the waiter. Mollie looked cross.

"I'm not butting in, am I?" I asked.

"Now why should you think that?" she said ambiguously.

I grinned at Mellor. "You want to be careful what you say to this young woman," I said. "The *Courier's* a sensational rag—always ruining reputations."

"As a matter of fact," Mollie said, "we were talking about motor cars. I'm not on duty every moment of the day, you know."

"My mistake," I said. "You must have changed!" I glanced towards the door, expecting to see Gloria come in at any moment, but she didn't. "What's happened to Miss Drage?" I asked

Mellor's handsome face turned slightly pink under its tan, and he looked very sheepish. "I'm afraid she's left," he said.

"Left?"

"Yes—she's gone back to London. We—er—had a bit of a quarrel."

"Never mind," Mollie said soothingly to Mellor, "you know very well she wasn't your type." She gave him a quite devastating smile, a real come-hither smile. "I have a feeling you're not going to miss her."

I could scarcely believe my ears. I stared at Mollie, but she was still looking at Mellor. After a moment I said, "What happened?"

"Well," Mellor said, "she was very annoyed because I insisted on going to see Anstey this morning. She said all I cared about was the boat and that she was fed up—and then she went off and packed. The next thing I knew she'd called a taxi and left me flat."

"Surely not *flat?*" Mollie said, ogling him over the edge of her glass. "I think that's very ungallant of you, Guy . . ."

So it was "Guy", now! I began to feel pretty annoyed, and for two pins I'd have left, but my drink had arrived and Mellor seemed quite glad to have me around. I said, "Cheers!" to Mellor, and asked him what he planned to do now, and he said he hadn't decided anything definite but he thought he'd do a bit of exploring around Cornwall now he was here. Mollie broke in and said she'd discovered a wonderful cove that morning and why didn't they go swimming some time, and he said that would be very nice, without any great enthusiasm. We talked a bit about Cornwall, and a bit about sailing, and then I suggested another drink. Mellor hesitated. "Thanks—but I think another time, if you don't mind. It's been quite a day—I'd like to get an early night."

Mollie said, "Oh, come on, Guy!—just one more."

"No, really—I'm pretty tired."

"Well, I'll be seeing you, then—won't I? Don't forget you promised to show me the Bentley's engine."

He gave a slightly embarrassed smile. "I won't forget. Good

night, Mollie. Good night, Curtis!" And he went out.

There was a short, frosty silence. Then I said, "What's the idea, Mollie?"

"I don't know what you mean," she said.

"No? Why, you did everything except play footy with him! Maybe you did that, too! What are you up to?"

"I'm not up to anything," she said. "I just find him rather fascinating, that's all."

"You're not serious!"

"Why shouldn't I be?"

"The chap's a wolf."

"I don't know why you should say that. He hasn't been a wolf with me. Rather the reverse."

"My dear innocent, that's just his technique ... Anyway, he didn't need to be, with you throwing yourself at his head all the time."

"If I was," she said, "I don't know that it has anything to do with you."

"The fellow's a womaniser," I said angrily, "anyone can see that. Damn it, he's just got rid of one tart and now ..."

"Don't say it!"

"And you know I want to marry you," I finished lamely.

She made no reply to that. She just picked up her bag, and got up to leave. At the door she turned, and gave me a little wave, and a very nice smile. I lit a cigarette and sat on in the bar till closing time, wondering whether she was crazy or whether I was.

Chapter Nine

The story looked deader than ever when I went in to breakfast next morning. The newspapers, without exception, carried brief and scrappy pieces. The message that Lawson and I had sent had been cut to ribbons. What was worse, I couldn't think of a single new approach to the case. I should have to keep in touch with Anstey, of course, but otherwise the day stretched emptily ahead as far as getting any real news was concerned. Perhaps, after all, Lawson had had a better break than he'd realised.

I wondered what the other reporters would be doing—those who hadn't already been recalled. I looked out of the dining-room window to see what Press cars were still in the square. Mollie's Sunbeam Talbot was parked right opposite me—she, at least, was still around. I wondered if she had a hangover today—too much whisky seemed the most charitable explanation of her behaviour the night before. It wasn't credible, I told myself, that she could really have fallen for Mellor's toothpaste smile.

A clock in the square struck nine. As the last note died, I saw Mollie come out of her hotel and walk briskly to her car. No sign of a hangover there! No sense of story anticlimax, either. She looked alert and purposeful. I watched her drive in to the filling station across the road. Judging by the time it took the man to operate the pump, she was taking a lot of petrol aboard. While she waited, she sat studying the map. Afterwards she had the man check her oil and tyres. It looked as though she planned to go farther than police headquarters. My professional antennae registered curiosity and mild anxiety. "Keep your eye on Mollie!" Lawson had said. Perhaps this was the moment.

I went out to the Riley. She saw me, and acknowledged my waved greeting, but she showed no inclination to stop and talk. In fact, the speed with which she drove off directly the man bad finished suggested violent avoiding action. For a second or two I hesitated. Blair would probably be coming through on the phone soon after eleven, perhaps with fresh instructions. Still, he could leave a message—and it was my story now, to handle in my own way. If Mollie could take time off for a drive, there was no reason why I shouldn't. I got into the Riley and set off after the Sunbeam Talbot.

With its conspicuous coachwork, it was an easy car to keep in sight. Now that Mollie was away she seemed in no great hurry, and I dawdled along behind her, keeping well out of driving-mirror range. People were still going to work, and there was quite a lot of traffic on the road out of Falmouth, which helped. I closed up a little as we approached the lights at the Helston-Truro crossing. She slipped through, turning right towards Truro. I had to wait. By the time I'd caught up again, there was another car between her and me, travelling at the same pace, which was ideal. It was a most attractive road, and driving in the warm sunshine was very pleasant. I began to feel much more cheerful.

I closed up again as we entered Truro, to avoid losing her in the busy town. There were three cars between us now, but I had no difficulty in keeping her in sight. Then, just outside the town, she forked left, heading north along a quieter road, and I had to drop back. We covered six miles uneventfully, and then joined A 30 the main London-Land's End artery. The Sunbeam Talbot turned towards London, and suddenly Mollie opened up.

For the next fifteen miles it was all I could do to keep pace with her. She was a first-class driver, with a newer car, and she had the edge on me in nipping past lorries. Much of the time we were both doing well over seventy, and it seemed only a matter of minutes before we were in Bodmin. There, I got badly stuck behind a huge lorry drawing a tree trunk, and lost her altogether. I had to gamble that she was still on A 30, but it turned out all right for I picked up her tail again as we began the long pull up on to Bodmin moor.

She was still going very fast, and I began to feel a bit anxious about where I was going to end up. She hadn't got her luggage with her, so there couldn't be any question of her going back to town—but I should feel pretty foolish if it turned out she'd been given the day off and was visiting some West Country aunt! Yet reporters working alone on important out-of-town stories just didn't get days off, I told myself. Whatever she was doing must be strictly business.

We were well up on the moors, now, and the undulating road, stretching away across nearly twenty miles of wild and almost uninhabited country, was most inviting. The rugged slopes of the hills on either side were a blaze of heather, and the tors looked magnificent against the deep blue of the sky. The air smelt divine.

I roared up a long slope to one of the road's highest points, slowed a little as I topped the rise, and looked ahead to see where the Sunbeam Talbot had got to. Then I saw something else, and braked hard, scarcely able to believe my eyes. There was a car drawn up on the grass verge—an unmistakable car. It was Mellor's old Bentley!

For a second I felt a surge of wild, unreasoning jealousy. The car was empty, but Mellor must obviously be somewhere close at hand, and it couldn't possibly be a coincidence. Mollie must have made a tryst with the blighter! I gazed ahead, but there was a dip in the road, and I couldn't see him, or the Sunbeam Talbot either. I rammed the gear in and trod on the gas. Almost at once I was over the dip and there was a clear view of the road for the best part of a mile ahead and I still couldn't see anyone. The Sunbeam Talbot seemed to have vanished. I slowed again, baffled. It couldn't have covered that distance in a few seconds—and there was nothing to block the view, not even a tree. Then as I trickled along, looking to right and left, I came to a place where a bit of the moor had been quarried out at the side of the road—and there was Mollie's car, in the quarry. She was still sitting in it, by herself. I turned in and parked alongside.

For a moment she just stared at me in astonishment. Then she said, in a haughty, spoiled-darling-of-the-*Courier* voice, "I suppose

I'm following you again!"

I was inwardly seething, but there didn't seem much I could do. I couldn't even think of anything to say now that I was here. If she was so smitten with the fellow that she'd made a secret assignation with him, the only dignified thing I could do was to take myself off and leave her to it. I re-started the engine and put the gear into reverse. "If I'd known you were meeting Mellor," I said, "I wouldn't have come. I'm afraid it never occurred to me."

"I'm not meeting him," she said.

"But . . ."

"He just happens to interest me, that's all," She took a mirror from her bag, examined her face, and removed a speck of dust with the corner of her handkerchief. "In a purely professional way."

"Really?. . . I'd have said your interest went well beyond the call of duty."

"Well, you'd be wrong."

"Then why on earth didn't you say so last night?"

"For one thing," she said, "you looked so beastly proprietorial I just couldn't take it."

"Oh!" I switched off the engine. "Anyway, what's interesting about him?"

"Perhaps you'd like to see a carbon copy of all my stories from now on?" she said.

It was an old gag between us, but I smiled just the same. "Still war to the knife, is it? Okay, I can take a hint." I reached for the ignition key.

"You're like someone with St. Vitus's Dance," she said. "Why don't you relax for a moment?"

"You know I don't want to muscle in . . ."

"On the contrary, I know there's nothing you'd like better—isn't that what you came for? But as it happens there's probably nothing to muscle in on—it's just a hunch I had, and it's too libellous to use, anyway. I simply wondered if Mellor was quite what he seemed to be, that's all."

"Why?—don't you believe his story?"

"I don't disbelieve it. I just wondered. He could be involved in this thing, you know."

"I don't see how. He certainly couldn't have been one of the raiders—not if he was in Belgium."

"No, but he might be in cahoots with them. He might have agreed to let them use his boat—in return for a 'cut'. That would explain how they were able to go off in her so confidently."

"Oh—you thought of that too, did you?"

"Naturally."

"Well," I said, "if he *was* in with them he'd have known that he wouldn't find his boat in the creek when he got here—in fact, he couldn't ever have intended to go on his Scillies trip."

"Perhaps he didn't. Perhaps it was just an excuse to bring the boat down here."

"All I can say is, he went to an awful lot of trouble . . ."

"I wouldn't say so. It doesn't take long to dump a few provisions in a car and buy a chart or two."

"What about Gloria?" I said. "If he'd known all the time that he wasn't going to make the trip, would he have dragged her into it?"

"He might. After all, she makes the whole thing more convincing."

"She's been quite a headache to him. He told me the publicity would probably ruin the rest of his love-life."

"I imagine he'll get by."

"H'm! Well, my impression was that he was genuinely worried—about Gloria, about the boat, about everything . . . What started you off on this line, anyway?"

"To be quite honest," she said, after a slight pause, "his attitude to me. He doesn't seem to want to have anything to do with me."

"That makes him a crook, for sure!" I said.

She laughed. "I know it sounds silly—but just consider. He came down here for a holiday, a good time. He's obviously not indifferent to women. His own girl friend's abandoned him. He's nothing much to do except check with the police occasionally to see if there's any news of his boat. In fact, he's really quite at a loose end. But when I throw myself at his head, as you put it, tell him I'm interested in his car, suggest we go swimming together, all that sort of thing—he shies right away. Why?"

"He doesn't find you attractive."

"If you believe that," she said, "of course there's nothing more to discuss."

I didn't believe it.

I said, "Perhaps you piled on the pressure too much. Men do like to pick their own girls, you know."

She shook her head. "I didn't pile on the pressure to start with. I was just ordinarily nice to him, and he still shied. That rather surprised me, so I really did begin to hang around him then, just to see what it was all about."

"What do you think it *is* all about?"

"I think he wants to be left on his own—and I'd like to know why. That's why I'm keeping an eye on him."

"He wouldn't have been on his own if his girl friend hadn't left," I said. "And he could hardly have known she was going to rush off in a tantrum."

"I'm not so sure. We don't know who started that quarrel. Perhaps *he* did."

I grinned." You remind me of Lawson."

"Thanks!"

"In some ways . . . Honestly, though, there's not much evidence against Mellor, is there?"

"There's none at all. I told you, it's a hunch."

"M'm! What's he doing here now, anyway?"

"He's walking on the moor. I caught sight of him just after I'd passed his car."

"You knew he was coming, of course?"

"Of course."

"Well," I said, "it hardly looks as though he's got much to hide to-day if he told you his plans."

"He didn't tell me. All he said was that he was going to walk somewhere."

"Then how did you know he would come here?"

"He was looking at an inch-to-the-mile map when I joined him in the pub last night. He folded it up when he saw me and put it in his pocket, but the number was still visible—136, Ordnance Survey. That turned out to be the Bodmin sheet—and where else would he walk but the moor?"

"Very clever," I said. "But I certainly don't see anything sinister about it. He's been talking about walking, all along. He's obviously an open-air type—when he's not wolfing!"

"It seems a long way to come for a walk," Mollie said.

"Not with a car—and from Falmouth, it's about the nearest stretch of really open country . . . What do you imagine he's doing out there beside walking?"

"I don't know—meeting someone, perhaps . . . He might even be collecting his share of the loot!"

"What an imagination!" I picked up the binoculars and climbed out of the quarry. "Which direction was he going in?"

"Up towards the high tors," she said.

I could see the tors, two of them, their tops jutting sharp and clear above the gentler line of the foothills. They looked quite a long way away, and the intervening ground was rough. I swept the lower slopes with the glasses, and presently I spotted him. He was about a quarter of a mile away across the heather, climbing slowly. As I watched, he turned for a moment and gazed back over what must already have been quite a view.

I dropped down into the quarry again. "Well, he looks genuine enough to me," I said. "Anyway, what are you going to do about him? You can't keep an eye on him from here."

"I'm going to follow him, of course," Mollie said, and got out of the car. I noticed that she was wearing a pair of stout walking shoes. "You don't have to come if you don't want to."

"Do you mind if I do?"

"Not now you're here."

I gazed around. It was a lovely morning, and the moors looked most inviting.

"Then I think I'll come," I said, "as you're so pressing!"

Chapter Ten

I had a look at the car map before we set off. It was a poor substitute for an inch-to-the-mile, but it showed enough to leave little doubt where Mellor was making for. He was heading, as any hiker would, for the dominating tors, and I thought his objective would probably be the nearer one, called Brown Willy, which was shown on the map as 1,375 feet and was the highest point on the moor. From where we stood, it was a little over two and a half miles in a straight line. It would be quite a hike, but we were already nine hundred feet up so the climb wouldn't amount to much. In an hour and a half, at most, we should be there.

We reparked the cars, placing my less conspicuous Riley between Mollie's and the road in case Mellor should drive past the quarry or turn there when he came down. Then I slung the binoculars over my shoulder, and we set off. At first we dropped down a little, skirting a stone farmhouse with a few hedged fields. Then we followed a contour north-westwards above a trickling stream that the map had shown as the beginning of the River Fowey. Mollie left it to me to pick the route. The going was pretty rough all the way. Sometimes a sheep track happened to coincide with our direction for a while, but mostly we just ploughed through the heather and bracken on the sides of our feet. The long dry spell had baked the peaty ground on the hillside, which helped quite a lot. The air was very warm, and deliciously scented. There was a summer murmur of insects, a whirring of grasshoppers at our feet, a skylark or two trilling away above us, the occasional bleat of a sheep. That was all. Back on the ribbon of road, cars and lorries were still roaring by, but the sound was already muted. Very few of the cars stopped, I noticed, and even when they did the occupants rarely moved more than fifty yards from their seats. Before long, it was as though Mollie and I had the world to ourselves. I had no complaints. When I thought how unpromisingly the day had started, I could scarcely believe in my good fortune.

For the time being, there was little danger that Mellor would see us. He had taken a slightly more direct, but also a more undulating route than ours, and for much of the way he was hidden from us by an intervening tor. When, occasionally, he did reappear, we exercised care—though I thought he was too far ahead to have any chance of identifying us. He didn't seem to be carrying any glasses. He had a haversack on his back, and a stick in his hand, and to me he looked every inch the walker. I couldn't even begin to take Mollie's theory seriously, but at least it was giving us a splendid morning out.

We continued for a mile and a half along the contour, and then dropped down to cross the stream. It was very marshy in the valley, with treacherous patches of bright moss and a lot of cotton grass, and we got pretty well bogged down for a while. But we struggled out, and after a short rest we started the last stretch of the climb to the tor. We had to be very cautious now, for we were approaching within recognisable distance of Mellor, and on the one-in-a-thousand chance that he was up to something, there was no point in putting him on his guard. In any case, it would have been distinctly embarrassing if he'd recognised us. As we approached each fresh brow, we kept our heads down and moved very slowly until we made sure we were still below his line of vision. Apart from an occasional gorse bush, there was virtually no cover.

The climb grew steeper. By now, we were only a few hundred yards from the tor. At close quarters it looked most impressive, with its great pile of rocks black against the sky. Mellor must already have reached it. We advanced with infinite care, stalking rather than walking. Suddenly, as we breasted yet another of the numerous false tops, I caught sight of his head—fortunately, turned away from us. I grabbed Mollie and pulled her down beside me in the heather. After a moment we peered out through the purple tufts. We were well concealed as long as we didn't go any higher, but we hadn't a very good view. Mellor had seated himself right at the summit, with his back against a lump of granite, so that all we could see was his head.

"At least," Mollie said, "you've got to admit it makes a splendid rendezvous for anyone who wants to be sure of privacy!"

That was certainly true. Up there on the tor, with nothing higher to command it, and a clear view over the moors for miles in all directions, security would seem complete. It was frustrating not to be able to get nearer. For all we knew, Mellor had already joined somebody up there—someone who was sitting beside him just over the rocky horizon. I didn't believe it, but I'd have liked to make sure. As it was, we were too far away even to catch a murmur of voices. We tried working our way round the shoulder of the hill to see if we could find a better approach, but we couldn't—on the last stretch to the summit there was nothing to give concealment anywhere. We debated what to do. The two of us, even if we separated, could cover visually only a very small sector of the hill, so it seemed hardly worth while to take up different positions in the hope that a second man would descend in someone's line of vision and prove Mollie's point. It was better, we decided, to keep watch on Mellor, in the hope that by some gesture he would give away the presence of another man. Or we might even see another head! And, as Mollie said, we could hurry to the top when he left and see if anyone else was on the move.

We returned to our former look-out and lay down again. Mellor's head was still just visible. For a while we both watched him, but it was an unrewarding occupation, and presently Mollie relaxed in the sun and left the job to me. I continued to keep an eye on him, in a desultory sort of way. Once, through the glasses, I thought I saw his lips moving, and as I began to concentrate Mollie said, "What's he doing?" But it was a false alarm. "He's chewing," I said. "The blighter's having a snack ... Now he's drinking from a bottle."

"I wish we were," Mollie said.

I put the binoculars down and stretched out in the heather beside her. As I lay there, quietly sunning myself, I thought of the last time we'd been close together like this on a sloping bank—back in May. That had been another vigil we'd been keeping—only then it had been dark. Perhaps that was why she'd been so unexpectedly responsive when I'd started to get amorous. I wondered. I turned my head, and saw that she was looking at me. Her face seemed to have lost the aloof, faintly mocking expression that I always associated with Mollie when we were on the same story. It had quite a different expression, as though all her guards had dropped. I changed my position slightly, until my face was very close to hers, and she didn't move away. She just regarded me gravely. I kissed her mouth, and put my arms around her, and for a moment she lay there passively, letting me kiss her. Then she put her arms round me, too, and kissed me in return, and I wasn't interested in time-and-motion studies any more . . .

I'd have liked it to go on for ever, but it didn't. As I began to warm up, she gave a little sigh and gently pushed me away. "Better not start anything you can't finish," she said.

Reluctantly, I let her go. "Why is it you only become human when you're out on a hillside with me waiting for something to happen?" I asked her.

She smiled. "It's the slippery slope," she said. "I must try to keep on the level . . .! How's Mellor getting on?"

I'd quite forgotten him. I raised my head cautiously and looked up towards the tor. Then I ducked. "I think he's coming down," I said. Mollie looked, too, and suddenly gave a sharp exclamation. "Heavens, he's coming down this way!"

It was true—he was coming straight towards us, plunging down the slope with long, vigorous strides. If he hadn't spotted us already, he would at any moment—and he'd recognise Mollie if he didn't recognise me. That chestnut hair of hers wasn't a thing anyone could forget. There was nothing for it but to go into a clinch again. I flung myself on her, covering her head, pressing her body down into the heather. She lay there passively. The heavy, crunching steps drew nearer.

"Can't you be more passionate?" I whispered. "Don't forget

we're supposed to be miles from anyone."

She moved her head slightly and bit my ear so hard that I almost cried out.

"Darling!" she murmured.

The footsteps stopped—he must have seen us. Then they started again, in a different direction. After a moment or two, I raised my head. He was fifty yards down the slope, and going strong.

"Do you mind," Mollie said, "you're an awful weight!" I rolled off her, and she sat up, breathing hard, and brushed back her hair with her hand. "You do rather take advantage, don't you?"

"Just presence of mind in a crisis," I said. "Did you hear the clank of jewels as he passed? Fascinating sound!"

"Idiot! Anyway, we can go up now and look around."

"Better wait a bit," I said. "Let him get clear first."

We waited, watching Mellor. He stopped once or twice, but he didn't look back. The route ahead was all he seemed interested in. Presently he reached the stream, and got bogged down the way we had, and after that he was fully occupied extricating himself. It seemed safe to move. I gave Mollie a hand and we made a quick dash up the last fifty yards of the slope and reached the summit. We gazed around the tumbled rocks, but there was no one there. We looked down the hillside, but there was no one in sight.

I couldn't have been less surprised.

"Never mind," I said, "it's been a pleasant outing. Let's come again to-morrow!"

Mollie didn't reply. She was looking across the sweep of moors to the north-east where, two miles or more away, a thin strip of white road showed up against the heather. "What's that thing shining?" she said, and pointed. "Isn't that a car?"

I unhitched the binoculars, and had a look. It was a car, all right—the windscreen was reflecting the sun like a mirror. At that distance I couldn't make out any details. The road seemed to be a very minor one, and there was no other traffic.

"Probably a picnic party," I said. "It is August, after all."

"Can you see anyone?"

I had another look, but I couldn't. The car appeared to be empty, and there was no one near it on the verge. I swung the glasses back over the moor and slowly explored its undulations. I was about to report that there was nothing at all to be seen except sheep when, from a dip in the ground, a man's head appeared, and then his shoulders, and then all of him. He was walking at a steady pace in the direction of the car. He was at least a mile away from us, and for all I could make out he might have been anyone. I gave Mollie the glasses, and she had a look for herself.

"Well, there you are," she said after a moment, "there *is* someone. And going in the right direction. How do we know he didn't meet Mellor here, and leave first?"

"He's much more likely to be just another chap walking on the moor," I said. "It's no good, Mollie, we haven't proved a thing."

"Maybe not," she said, thoughtfully, as we turned to descend the hill. "But a hunch is a hunch."

Chapter Eleven

The morning had been so enjoyable that I began to hope Mollie would forget about being the hard-boiled reporter for a while and stick around with me. But I was disappointed. We were no sooner back in Falmouth than she called out, "Well, good hunting, Hugh!" and slipped away on her own. At once, I began to feel uneasy. I still had no faith in her hunch, but I wished she hadn't had it, all the same. She, at least, had an idea to pursue. I had nothing. It was an uncomfortably familiar feeling at this stage of a story, and I knew I should open the *Courier* next morning with more than my usual anxiety, in case it turned out that she'd stumbled on something big and hit the headlines. It had happened before like that, and there was always hell to pay at the *Record* afterwards, with Blair sulking and Hatcher treating me like a pariah. I wished there was some way of demolishing her hunch, so that I could forget it, but I couldn't think of one. The idea did cross my mind that I might try and check whether Mellor had received any letters or telephone calls at his hotel, by which an assignation on Bodmin Moor could have been made, but on reflection I decided he could easily have slipped out and telephoned someone himself, so the absence of an incoming message would mean nothing. Another possibility was to ask the office to try and trace Gloria Drage and get her version of the quarrel with Mellor, but it would mean involved explanations on the phone and I didn't think they'd take very kindly to the idea without far better grounds than I could give them. The plain fact was that, after what I'd seen of Gloria, Mellor's story had rung pretty true to me.

I had something to eat, and then went along to the quay and

rowed myself out to *Wanderer* to see if by any chance Attwood had any fresh ideas. But he wasn't even there. Apparently he'd decided to call off the Riviera trip for the time being, and he and his party had all returned to London that morning. *Wanderer* Harris said, would be sailing for the Solent in a few days. I wished him a good trip, and rowed back, and walked over to police headquarters. Everything was depressingly quiet there, too. Practically all the London reporters, it seemed, had gone back to town, leaving what was left of the story to the local men. Anstey was out, and his sergeant had no information about anything. I asked him what was being done about the gumboot prints, and he said inquiries were going on, but as practically everybody had gumboots these days there wasn't much hope of finding the right ones until they had some other lead.

I was just leaving when Mellor drove up. I told him Anstey was out, and that there was still no news of *Mary Ann*, or of anything else, and he pulled a long face. He was quite friendly—obviously he hadn't the slightest notion that he'd already seen me that day on the hillside—and I no longer felt any animosity towards him now that Mollie's motives had been made clear. I asked him how he was getting on and he said he'd spent a delightful morning walking on Bodmin Moor, a place he'd always intended to visit. He asked me if I'd ever been there, and I said "No", and he said I should because there was a fine view from the top of a tor called Brown Willy, only of course you had to like desolate country, which he did. He was most enthusiastic.

As we crossed the pavement to the Bentley I noticed that his suitcase was lying on top of the junk that was still piled in the back.

"Are you leaving?" I asked, in surprise.

"I've left the pub," he said, "that's all. It's too stuffy for me. I thought I'd do a bit of camping—after all, I might just as well eat my way through these tins as take them back, and the weather's just right for it."

"Have you got a tent?"

"I've just bought one." He patted a long, canvas-covered roll.

"A very neat job, and remarkably cheap. Not up to a boat's cabin for comfort, but I think I'll prefer it to flowered wallpaper!"

"Where are you going to pitch camp?"

"I don't know yet—not too far away, if I'm to keep in touch with Anstey. I'll have to take a look round."

"Almost anywhere along the cliffs would be pretty good, I should think. You'd get some swimming, too."

"Yes, that's an idea." He nodded affably. "I dare say I'll be seeing you."

"I expect so. If you're in Falmouth, look in at the Anchor some time and we'll have that drink."

"Good idea—I will." He opened the car door, then turned and gave me an odd look. "I say, that girl reporter's a bit of a menace, isn't she?"

"In what way?"

"Why, she's been positively haunting me. I reckon she needs a man."

"Don't you think she's attractive?"

He grinned. "She's attractive, all right, but personally I'm in enough woman trouble already . . . Ah, well—so long!" He climbed into the Bentley and drove off with a fine exhaust roar.

I walked slowly back towards the pub. As I turned into the square, I caught sight of Mollie. She was strolling along in a very leisurely way, looking in shop windows. I crossed the road and joined her.

"You don't seem to be very busy," I said.

"I'm not."

"Have you phoned a story?"

"Just a couple of columns!" she said airily.

The words jarred on me, even though I knew she hadn't. At least, I thought I knew.

"As a matter of fact," she said, "I've decided to take a day or two off. It's rather nice down here."

"It's rather nice to be able to take a day or two off when you feel like it!" I said. "Any jobs going on the *Courier*?"

"I doubt it. We've rather high standards, you know."

I let that pass. "I suppose you know your chief suspect is going camping?"

"I ought to," she said smugly. "I've just helped him buy a tent."

"Oh!"

"I must say he didn't seem terribly grateful."

"He thinks you're trying to seduce him," I said.

"Really?"

"Yes, I've just been talking to him . . . Incidentally, I feel surer than ever that that Bodmin trip was genuine."

"It could be."

"What are you going to do?—watch for smoke signals rising from the hills?"

"Something like that," she said. She gave me a maddeningly complacent smile. "Oughtn't you to be phoning your office?"

I went into the pub and put in a call to London. I'd no story to dictate, so I asked to be put straight through to the Desk. Hatcher, the Night News Editor, answered.

"It's Curtis . . ." I began.

"Anything doing?" he demanded.

"Well, not very much as a matter of fact, but . . ."

"Then come back," he said abruptly, and hung up. I stood looking at the dead receiver, feeling pretty savage. Smee was undoubtedly right—Hatcher was a born murderer, if ever I'd met one. I went into the bar and had a drink and considered the situation. I didn't at all want to go back. It wasn't, I told myself, that I didn't trust Mollie with Mellor, even if she had helped him buy a tent and fixed herself a few days off. It wasn't that at all. It was simply, I told myself, that even a wrong hunch could sometimes lead to a right one, and Mollie might still hit on something big. I should be doing less than my duty if I didn't point this out to my employers. I had another drink to fortify myself, and then put in another call to the office.

"Yes?" Hatcher said, in a voice that almost severed the line.

"This is Curtis again," I said. "Look, I was going to tell you there has been one development here that might be quite interesting

83

... I think it might be worth while my hanging on for a bit."

"What is it?"

"Well, it's a bit hush-hush ..."

"Hush-hush my foot—you're not in the bloody Secret Service! What's the gist of it?"

"I can't tell you over the phone—it's difficult ..."

"Then you'd better come back where it's easy ..." Hatcher gave a loud snort. "Lawson says the story's over till they find the boat. Everyone else is back. What do you want, a holiday with pay?"

"Mollie Bourne's still here," I said, "and she's on to this thing, too ... I thought I'd better warn you, that's all."

There was a short silence. Then Hatcher said, "Hang on!" I hung on, sweating. I heard a rumble of voices. Then Blair came on the line. After Hatcher, he sounded sweetly reasonable.

"Hallo, Curtis! What's all this about Mollie Bourne?"

"She's hanging on," I said. "Snooping around like mad, all very secretive—but I think I know what she's up to."

"I see." Blair considered. "All right, Curtis, you'd better stay on for a bit—but keep in touch."

"I will," I said, and rang off.

I didn't have a very comfortable evening—I guess my conscience must have been troubling me. I'd put a fast one over on the office, and I'd half committed myself to a story I was pretty sure didn't exist. I felt even more uncomfortable next morning, because most of the papers weren't even mentioning the Attwood raid any more. What was worse, it looked as though I wasn't even going to enjoy the fruits of my deceit, for Mollie wasn't at her hotel and I couldn't find her anywhere. It wasn't until I called at police headquarters in the afternoon for the usual check with Anstey that our paths crossed. I found her sitting outside the station in her car, studying a map.

"Hallo," she said, "you still here?"

"Why shouldn't I be?"

"The story seems to be over."

"Well, I can watch for smoke signals too! Have you discovered where Mellor's camp is?"

She hesitated, then gave a little shrug. Obviously I'd find out in any case. "Yes," she said, "Anstey just told me. It's at a place called Penlo Cove, on the other side of the Helford river." With a delicately tinted fingernail, she indicated the spot on the map.

"And now," I said, "I suppose you're thinking of taking a run up there and having a look round?"

"I might."

"You know," I said, "the way you're going on, you could get into trouble."

"So could lots of girls, but most of them don't."

"I don't mean that—not entirely, anyway. You seem to forget a man has been murdered. There could be some pretty desperate characters around."

"I thought you were so sure Mellor was on the level."

"I am, but I could be wrong."

"In that case, I shall probably get a scoop."

"Or a posthumous award! Look, I've got a proposition to make. You share the hypothetical scoop with me, I'll share the hypothetical risk with you. What do you say?"

For a moment she didn't answer. Then, to my astonishment, she said, "All right—it's a deal."

I smiled. "Now I *know* you don't really believe in your hunch," I said.

Chapter Twelve

To reach Penlo, we had to make a fifteen mile trip round the head of the Helford river again. We skirted Gillan Creek once more, this time keeping to the south of it. The cove was a mile or so farther on. The road became very narrow as we approached the coast, and in the end it was no more than a cart track. It passed through a farmyard and petered out at a gate that opened on to a field of barley, sloping down towards the sea. There was a stile near the gate, and a path alongside the barley. At the bottom of the field there was a dry-stone wall, with another stile. Beyond was the untamed Cornish cliff-top—a spectacular fringe of granite-sown turf, bracken, gorse bushes, and wild, tumbled rocks, linking an endless line of coves.

Penlo Cove proved to be a particularly fine one. It lay on the south side of a long promontory, so that the grassy slopes above it commanded a view of sea and cliff extending for a mile or more along the coast. It had a tiny stream, running down a gulley that gave easy access from the clifftop to the beach, and judging by the many footmarks in the sand it was well-used by holiday-makers. As a camping spot it was ideal; as a base for a man supposedly engaged in some nefarious business, it seemed to me to be much too popular a place. My scepticism grew with every step.

It didn't take us long to find Mellor's tent. We caught sight of it, from some distance away, on a grassy ledge about fifty feet above the beach. I turned my glasses on it, but there was no sign of Mellor. We'd rather expected that, as we hadn't seen his car parked anywhere. It made it easy for us to have a look round.

The camp was all that a camp should be. The tent was small, but there was ample room for one person. The site was bone dry. Thick gorse bushes to the north and east gave it some protection in case a fresh breeze should get up. The tent itself opened on to a breathtakingly lovely seascape to the south. Everything had been left very tidily. The heavier camp equipment was mostly tucked away behind some rocks—a four-gallon can of drinking water, a can of paraffin, a new-looking pressure stove, and a stack of tinned food. The flaps of the tent were closed, but there was a gap between them and we took a look inside. There was a neatly-folded sleeping-bag, and a pillow; a suitcase and a kitbag; a pile of paper-backed thrillers, and a small portable radio. Various other belongings were ranged around the edges of the tent. Mellor must have had quite a job, I thought humping all his stuff across the barley field, but I could well believe he'd found the effort, worth while. I'd have camped there with great pleasure myself.

I grinned at Mollie. "All frightfully suspicious, isn't it?"

She gave a faint shrug. "It looks all right—but I wouldn't mind having a quick look inside now we're here, all the same."

"Tent-breaking probably ranks with house-breaking," I said.

"I don't care—we'll never have a better chance to check on him ... Keep watch, will you, I'm going in."

I wasn't very happy about it, but she was already undoing the flaps. A moment later she'd slipped inside and was trying to open the suitcase. It was locked, but the kitbag wasn't, and she began to investigate its contents. I left her to it, and climbed to a strategic point above the camp, and looked carefully around. Two hikers were crossing the promontory, but they were still some distance away. From the beach below came the voices of children, playing. I hoped they'd stay there and not come rushing up. It would be pretty awkward if Mellor heard that a girl with red hair had been ransacking his belongings. Almost as bad as if he suddenly returned and caught us in the act. At the thought of that, I walked up to the stile and glanced across the field. But there was no sign of him. The two hikers had turned away inland. Presently I heard a halloo from Mollie and went down again to the tent. She was standing by the entrance, with a sheet of paper in her hand.

"Something interesting?" I said.

She gave a rueful smile. "You win, I'm afraid—that trip *was* on the level." She showed me the paper. It was a letter from Mellor's bank in London, and it was addressed to him at the hotel where he'd been staying in Falmouth. It said: "Thank you for your letter of August 18th. We note that you will not after all be using the withdrawal facilities arranged for you at our branch in St. Mary's, Isles of Scilly. In accordance with your request, we are asking our Falmouth branch to provide facilities there."

I handed it back to her. "Ah, well, you can't expect every hunch to come off—and at least you've eliminated him."

She nodded. "Unfortunately it doesn't leave anyone . . ." She put the letter back in its envelope and slipped the envelope between the pages of a book while I stood guard outside.

I said, "Was that letter marking his place, do you suppose?"

"If it was, it still is . . . Don't worry, everything's just as we found it." She closed the tent flaps, and we started back up the slope.

It was a beautiful evening, and I didn't at all want to leave. I knew only too well what would happen now. When I reported "no progress" to the office they'd obviously tell me to go back, and then—if past experience was anything to go by—it might be weeks before I saw Mollie again. I'd be crazy not to make the most of these last few hours. I glanced across at her. With Mellor off her mind, she wasn't looking quite so uncompromisingly professional as she had been doing. I said, "It's only half past five, Mollie—why don't we go for a walk?"

"We went for a walk yesterday," she said.

"Well, it's not a rationed exercise."

"It's not an exercise at all if you take it horizontally! Do you *mean* a walk?"

"I'm entirely in your hands . . . Anyway, you're off duty now—why not loosen up a bit?"

"The moment I loosen up with you," she said, "you try to put a half-Nelson on me . . .!" She stood for a moment gazing out over the sea, while a faint breeze gently stirred her hair. "Still, it is very lovely . . . All right, let's go."

We chose a promising path and set off southwards along the cliff. The heat of the day was passing, the air was fragrant with gorse and thyme, the sea was a forget me-not blue and so calm that even around the outlying rocks there was scarcely a ruffle of foam. There were several rowing boats out, and a couple of small yachts, almost stationary in the light airs. The scene couldn't have been pleasanter. We met a few people, but not enough to make the clifftop seem crowded. The path turned and twisted excitingly, sometimes climbing almost to the edge of the cultivated field, sometimes dropping down to sea level when a gulley broke the line of the towering cliffs. One cove succeeded another, each different from the last, and each calling for some exploration. Most of them were accessible after a bit of a scramble, through we came across one, about half a mile from our starting point, that was shown on the map as Hell's Mouth and that we couldn't get down to at all. Fearsome cliffs dropped precipitously to a jagged, rock-strewn beach, and even on a quite day like this it was an aweinspiring place. Then, beyond the next promontory, the scene softened again. There was a wide scimitar of sand, with several tracks leading down to it. The cove lay full in the evening sun and looked very inviting. A white motor cruiser had dropped its anchor at the entrance, and as she swung broadside on to us I recognised her. She was *Curlew*—the boat whose occupants had given me the interview I hadn't used. Mollie hadn't met them, but she remembered seeing the boat.

I turned my glasses on to the cruiser. After a moment I said, "There doesn't seem to be anyone aboard her."

"There must be," Mollie said. "Her dinghy's alongside."

The boat swung a little further, and I could see down into the cockpit and right through the open door into the saloon, and I still couldn't see anyone. "I expect they've swung ashore," I said. "Probably sunning themselves on the rocks."

Mollie took the glasses and idly scanned the boulders that lined the cove. "I don't see them . . ." She looked up and gave me a mischievous smile. "Do you suppose she's another *Marie Celeste*?"

"You're off duty," I reminded her. "Let's go down on the beach and paddle."

We scrambled down the side of the cove and picked our way over lichened rocks to the sand. It was firm and smooth and still warm from the sun, and where the wavelets flowed over it it had a lovely sheen. Mollie slipped her shoes and stockings off and I rolled up my trousers and we splashed in and out along the tired of that we explored the dripping entrance of a cave under a cliff, where the rock had fascinating veins of pinkish marble, and watched the fish darting in shallow pools where mussels hung in clusters like black grapes; and Mollie gathered some sea shells for a small niece. Then we climbed the arm of the cliff on the other side of the cove and sat down to smoke a cigarette before returning to the car.

I was just lighting Mollie's for her when she gave sudden exclamation and pointed out over the water towards *Curlew*. "Look!"

I looked, and gaped. Close beside the cruiser's short ladder a head had come up out of the water—a head with a glass-covered face mask on it. A man with a very brown torso pulled himself up slowly, climbed aboard, and removed the mask. I recognised John Thornton. He had some breathing apparatus strapped to his back.

He was followed almost at once by a plumper and pinker man—Blake—similarly equipped.

"Well!—what do you know!" I said. "They've been aqualunging. That's why we didn't see them." It was a possibility that simply hadn't occurred to me—though it should have done. I could see, now, that there were lines of bubbles across the entrance to the cove.

"They must be pretty tough," Mollie said, "they've been down a long time." She looked at her watch. "It's nearly three quarters of an hour since we first saw the boat."

"Is that a long time?"

"It's a long time for English waters, I'd have thought."

"The sea's warmer than usual."

"It wouldn't feel very warm after you'd been skin-diving for a while."

"You sound very knowledgeable," I said. "Have you ever tried it?"

"I did quite a bit of diving with a mask and a schnorkel tube at Porquerolles last summer."

"Is there anything you haven't done?"

She smiled demurely. "Yes," she said.

"Is it fun—skin-diving, I mean?"

"Wonderful—especially in the Mediterranean. The colours are so marvellous there. And it's quite amazing what you can see under water with a mask on."

One of the men—Thornton—was looking across at us. He evidently recognised me, for he gave a cheery wave. I waved back. He stood leaning against the side of the cockpit for a while, chatting to Blake. They still had their aqualungs on. Presently they went into the saloon and emerged with two long, pointed things that I thought at first were fishing rods but that turned out to be harpoon guns when I studied them through the glasses. They loaded them, and adjusted their masks, and lowered themselves overboard again.

"They *are* gluttons for punishment," Mollie said.

"What do you suppose they expect to shoot?"

"Fish, of course." She seemed a trifle preoccupied.

"I know that," I said, "but I wouldn't have thought there'd be anything very rewarding so close in."

"In France," Mollie said, frowning, "it's illegal to hunt with aqualung equipment."

"Oh?—why?"

"Well, it's too easy to make a big haul if you don't have to come up for air—it doesn't give the fish enough chance. I'm sure it's not considered at all sporting here, either."

"Those cads can't have heard," I said.

I watched, fascinated, as fresh lines of bubbles spread over the water. This time, though, the divers didn't stay down long. After about ten minutes the bubble tracks approached the boat and they both climbed out once more. Blake didn't seem to have used his gun, but Thornton had harpooned one very small fish.

"*They* haven't reduced the underwater population very much, anyway," I said.

"Perhaps they're not very experienced."

They were unhitching the aqualungs, now, and beginning to towel themselves. Presently Thornton went forward and got the anchor, and Blake started the engine after a bit of trouble, and then got under way. Thornton gave a parting wave, and then they were out of the cove and turning up the coast in the direction of the Helford river.

Mollie was still pensive. "You know," she said, gazing after them, "*I* think that was rather peculiar."

I looked at her in surprise. "What was?"

"Why, the whole thing. Spending all that time under water without guns—and then suddenly popping back in again *with* guns. They couldn't really have wanted to hunt at that stage, surely?"

I laughed. "They obviously did. Fishing chaps are unaccountable, everybody knows that. As for spending all that time under water, I imagine they were just exploring."

"There can't be much to explore out in the cove itself—and they didn't go anywhere near the rocks, which is where the interesting things always are. If they had we'd have seen the bubbles."

"They were practising, then."

"If you're practising, I'm sure you don't stay down three-quarters of an hour at a stretch."

I shrugged. "Well, what do *you* think they were doing?"

"I don't know—but I'd rather like to."

"You're beginning to look a bit trance-like," I said. "This isn't the start of some new hunch, is it?"

"Not really, but . . ." She broke off, hesitating. "Well, here we've been thinking for days about two crooks who must have had last-minute information about *Wanderer*, and now we come across two men whose boat was moored fairly near to *Wanderer*, and they behave as though they've something to cover up . . ."

"Oh, come!" I protested.

"Well, they behave strangely, anyway."

"I wouldn't say so—it seemed to me they were just enjoying themselves. Anyway, what are you suggesting?—that these two chaps went to all the trouble of pinching the jewels and then came here and chucked them overboard, or something?"

"I shouldn't think so—but I still say it's rather odd."

"It would be even odder," I said, "if you were right, and we'd happened to stumble on the very crooks we were after, during a casual evening stroll!"

"Coincidences do happen."

I took her arm and drew her up. "Let's go and get some dinner," I said. "I think you're just weak from lack of food!"

Chapter Thirteen

We dined together in Falmouth and for me, at any rate, that rounded off a pretty enjoyable day. Mollie was in rather a quiet mood—she said the fresh air had made her sleepy—and she went off shortly after dinner, but before we parted she let me make a provisional date with her for a Saturday evening in town, which was more than she'd ever done before in advance. After she'd gone I rang the office to tell them the idea I'd been working on hadn't come to anything. I was prepared for a nasty crack or two from Hatcher, but as it happened I didn't have to speak to him. He was at supper, and Lawson was temporarily in charge of the Desk. Lawson said he trusted I'd had a good time and I said I had but all good things came to an end and this one had, and then he rang Hatcher on another phone and confirmed that I was to go back.

"Hatcher says ring us to-morrow night when you get in," he said. "Cheerio, old boy—my regards to your Moll!"

I made a mental note to beat him to a pulp when I next saw him, and rang off. Soon afterwards I turned in.

I woke to another exquisite morning—very still, and very warm, with an almost cloudless sky. The barometer in the hotel lobby hadn't budged a millimetre. The thought of leaving Cornwall for London on such a day was most unappealing, but there wasn't anything I could do about it. I had breakfast and was just going up to my room to pack when I was called to the telephone.

It was Mollie.

"Oh!—you're still there!" she exclaimed in a tone of relief. "Hugh, I must see you—can you hang on for a little while?"

"What's happened?" I asked.

"It's a bit complicated—I'll tell you when I see you."

"Where are you?"

"I'm at Manaccan. I'm on my way back—I'll only be about half an hour."

"All right," I said, "don't break your neck. I'll wait."

"Thanks a lot. 'Bye." She hung up.

I looked at my watch and saw that it was still only a few minutes to nine. She must have gone out extraordinarily early. I was consumed with curiosity about what she'd been up to. She'd sounded as though she might have a new line on something—though if she had, I found it hard to believe she'd want to tell me about it.

I took the *Record* and the *Courier* into the lounge and settled down to wait. I'd just about finished them when she came hurrying in, her eyes bright with secret knowledge. She'd had no breakfast, so I ordered coffee and rolls for her and asked what all the excitement was about.

She said, "I went back to the cove this morning."

"Which cove?" I asked.

"The one where *Curlew* was anchored, of course."

"Really?—whatever for?"

"Just curiosity. And guess what I found there."

I grinned. "A diamond necklace, washed up on the beach!"

"Well, not exactly—but *Curlew* was back there, and those two men were diving again."

I said, "Oh!" non-committally.

"I thought they might be," she said, "so I went along early. It was a long shot, of course, but I just hadn't been able to sleep for thinking about them and the odd way they'd swum up and down all that time and then put on their little hunting act when they saw us. The more I thought about it, the more I had the feeling that they'd been *looking* for something, and if had they didn't seem to have found it, and I wondered if they'd go back again. And then I remembered that it been low tide when we'd seen them, which of course would be much better for diving because the water would be shallower, and I thought they might go back at low tide again. So I took a chance, and drove to the cove at crack of dawn, and I'd just arrived when *Curlew* showed up . . ." She broke off, slightly out of breath. "Don't you think it's all rather interesting?"

"I don't see that there's anything very sinister about it, if that's what you mean," I said. "They probably like that cove, and yachtsmen usually reckon to start the day early, and this morning must have been just right for a bit of fishing. Were they using their harpoon guns?"

"No, they weren't."

"Well—did you still have the impression they were looking for something . . .? Where were they diving?"

"It was mostly round the boat this time, as a matter of fact . . ."

"There you are, then. I'd say they were just enjoying their swim."

"They might have hit on the right spot to-day, and found what they were looking for straight away."

"Were they anchored in a different place?"

"I thought so. It's hard to judge from the shore, but they seemed to me to be quite a bit farther out."

"M'm . . .! Still, if they'd been looking for something, and they'd found it, surely they'd have brought it up at once . . . Or did they know you were watching them?"

"No, I don't think so—I kept hidden."

"So they wouldn't have had any reason not to . . ." I shook my head. "I bet they were just amusing themselves."

"If that's all they were doing," Mollie said, "there'd have been no special point in their going back at low tide, because they could easily have gone farther inshore and anchored in whatever depth of water they wanted for diving. But if they knew they had to search in a particular spot, the low tide aspect would have been quite important."

"It was probably pure chance that they came at low tide," I said. "Anyway, Mollie, you can't really believe that the jewels are in that cove—it's fantastic. Why *would* they be?"

"Because it's a good hiding place, I should think. Look, if those two on *Curlew* were the raiders, they'd be bound to realise there'd be inquiries at the anchorage, and they certainly wouldn't have wanted to take the jewel case back to their yacht after the raid.

They wouldn't have wanted to have it around at all, not till things had blown over a bit. And they wouldn't have wanted to leave Falmouth with it, either, in case their sudden absence drew attention to themselves. So the obvious thing would have been to hide it—and what better place could there be than the seabed? As long as they weighted the case, they'd know it would be absolutely safe."

"Not if a rough sea got up," I said. "Not unless it was made very secure."

"Then perhaps that's what they were doing this morning—making it secure. They might even have been burying it in the sand! That would explain why they didn't bring it up when they found it."

"But Mollie," I said, "it just doesn't square with the rest of the information we've got. How could Thornton and Blake possibly be the raiders, when we know that whoever did the job took *Mary Ann* off to sea afterwards? Those two were certainly back here early the following morning—even if they were away during the night."

"I know, I thought of that," Mollie said, "but there could easily be some explanation. For instance, suppose there was a third man involved in the raid—someone who'd stayed in *Mary Ann's* cabin all the time. He could have brought Thornton and Blake back in her, dumped the jewel case in the cove for safety, put them ashore, and then taken the boat away on his own."

"That would have given the R.A.F. planes hours longer to spot her," I said. "It's almost inconceivable that they wouldn't have seen her."

"If they didn't see her in four hours," Mollie said, "I don't see why they should have seen her in eight or twelve. All that part of the thing's a mystery, anyway. If you ask me, I think the raiders must have thought up some way of camouflaging her."

"They couldn't change her shape."

"They might have changed her colour, though. It wouldn't have taken long for three or four men to slap on a coat of white paint above the waterline, would it?"

I hadn't thought of that—but somehow it didn't sound very likely. In fact, Mollie's theory didn't sound very likely at all. I'd always supposed that *Mary Ann* had cleared off because the raiders had cleared off—and if they hadn't I didn't see any point in her flight. I recalled what little I knew about Thornton and Blake, and I couldn't think of any suspicious thing about them. When I'd seen them, they'd always been behaving like genuine holidaymakers. At the same time, they had been anchored strategically close to *Wanderer*, and it suddenly occurred to me that David Scott must have passed very near to them on his way to post his letter, so that if he'd been in the conspiracy he could easily have called out the sailing information they needed as he went by.

"Well," I said, finally, "I suppose it's *just* possible you may be on to something."

"*I* think it's possible," Mollie said, "because of the way those two behaved ..." For a moment she regarded me thoughtfully. Then she said, "Look, Hugh, why don't we try and check?"

"You mean, see if we can get a line on how Thornton and Blake spent that night, and what time they got back—that sort of thing?"

"No, I mean get hold of some masks and schnorkels and have a look at the bottom of the cove ourselves. That's the quick way."

I stared at her. "You're not serious?"

"I'm perfectly serious."

"But ... Well, for one thing, I'd be no use. I've never done any underwater diving."

"I don't suppose there'd be any need to dive—with masks on, we'd probably be able to see the bottom from the surface. If not, I could do the diving till you'd got used to it. You're a strong swimmer, it wouldn't take you any time at all to learn—and I'm sure you'd enjoy it."

"I dare say!—but you seem to forget I've been told to go back to town. If I ring up Hatcher to-night from here and tell him I've been spending the day schnorkelling he'll probably have me schnorkelled off the paper!"

"Not if you get a terrific story."

"*If!*"

"You might."

I looked at her eager face. "You know," I said, "there was a time when you'd have gone off and inspected the sea bed on your own. What's happened to you?"

"Well, it's always better to have a companion when you're diving."

"You'd better watch out, Mollie—I believe you're beginning to rely on me. Soon you won't be able to do without me at all. That's the day I'm waiting for!"

"Don't be silly—it's only that we did agree to share the scoop and the risks."

"That was when you still suspected Mellor—it was quite a different matter—and quite different risks! What about all those things that happen to divers—bends, nitrogen poisoning, bleeding from the ears ...?"

"They only happen if you go deep—they don't concern skin divers with schnorkels. There's practically no risk at all, actually. But of course, if you're nervous ..."

"You're damn' right I'm nervous," I said. "When you get this crazy sort of idea I'm always nervous—and on past form I've good reason to be! What's more, I'm pretty sure there's nothing in that cove to find—it's a thousand to one that we'll be wasting our time. And what'll I tell the office?"

"You could be ill."

"Oh, no! I was ill the last time you got me on one of these larks—they'll never swallow that one again."

"Well, you can easily make out a case—afterwards! The important thing is that you'll be showing initiative—and that's a quality newspapers always like."

I wasn't so sure. I sat silent for a while, looking out of the window, thinking about her theory. I probably *could* make out a case, of course. And it was certainly a lovely day!

"Well, I admit I'm tempted," I said at last. "As a matter of fact, there's nothing I'd like better than to go swimming with you ... Remember the last time?"

"To-day," she said firmly, "I shall be wearing a swimsuit."

"You look nice in a swimsuit too," I said. I fought with my conscience for about thirty seconds, and lost easily. "All right—you've talked me into it."

She jumped to her to feet. "Then let's go and see about equipment. There's a sports shop in the square with some masks in the window."

I followed her out in a slight daze.

Chapter Fourteen

The Man in the sports shop was knowledgeable and helpful. He had, he said, a good stock of supplies to meet the growing popularity of skin-diving in Cornwall, and he showed us his range. There was an astonishing variety of masks. Most of them were oval in shape, and all had unbreakable glass fronts, but some had bits shaped for the nose, some had lenses, and some had schnorkels already attached. In the end we chose the simplest kind, with the widest possible glass window to give good vision and soft rubber round the edge of the mask so that it didn't cut the face. We had to test them in the old wartime way, by breathing in gently through the nose when they were in position and making sure that the rubber sides were sucked in against the face. After that, Mollie and the shopman had a rather technical discussion about schnorkels, and whether it was better to have the sort with a valve or not, and we finally settled for two neat little plastic jobs that had a wide U-bend to clear the face and were open at the top. Then the shopman produced several enormous pairs of fins for our feet and we sat down and tried them on as gravely as though we were in a shoe shop, though we must have looked pretty funny. The whole kit cost several pounds. It would make, I thought, an unusual item on my expenses sheet if I ever dared to include it!

When we were fixed up, Mollie fetched a soft travelling bag from her car and we packed all the equipment away in it before we left the shop in order not to advertise what we were doing. Then we collected our swimming things, bought some food for a picnic lunch, and drove round the Helford river again in the Riley. I parked the car in the old spot beside the barley field and we set off along the top of the cliff with the gear still in the bag. At Mollie's suggestion we gave Curlew Cove, as we now called it, a wide berth for the moment, and for my initial practice chose another, smaller one, farther on, with a good strip of sand and a conveniently shelving beach. The scramble down the cliff at that point was severe enough to deter most holidaymakers, so that we had the place to ourselves. The sun was deliciously warm, and the sea was like glass. We changed quickly among the rocks, and met at the water's edge for my first lesson.

To begin with, Mollie said, I must get used to the feel of the equipment. I put the face mask on, covering my eyes and nose, and took the soft flange of the schnorkel mouthpiece between my lips and gums, as Mollie directed, and gripped the two lugs with my teeth. Then I spent a minute or two practising breathing. It was easy enough on dry land, except that it took me a little time to get the knack of closing my glottis and breathing only through my mouth, and at first the glass plate tended to mist up inside. When I'd got over that difficulty, we cleaned the plates with seaweed, rinsed the equipment, made sure the masks were watertight, fitted the fins, and waded into the sea until we stood waist-deep. With the schnorkel securely fastened to my mask strap by a rubber band, and the flange in my mouth, I dipped my head under the surface for my first underwater breathing test. It wasn't a very pleasant sensation to start with and I had to make a conscious effort to stay under, but as my breathing became more relaxed and regular the discomfort passed.

Then came the next stage—floating with my head just submerged and the top of the schnorkel tube sticking up an inch or two out of the water. The sense of imminent asphyxia came back more strongly, but again it didn't last. Most of it, I imagined, was just beginner's nerves. What wasn't nerves was when I went down a little farther than I meant to and a tiny wavelet lopped over the top of the schnorkel. In an instant I was spluttering and. gasping, with a flooded tube, a mouthful of water, and no breath. I emerged to find Mollie standing beside me with her mask pushed up over her swimming cap, shaking with laughter. When I'd stopped spluttering she assured me that everyone did the same thing to start with, and that I'd soon learn to blow the water out of the tube without choking. The important thing, she said, was to take everything quite camly. It was all very well for her, of course, but I had a strong feeling she was telescoping half a dozen lessons into one. However, it was all good fun.

We swam about in the cove for quite a while, and my confidence in the schnorkel steadily increased. What was more, I began to understand the tremendous attraction of underwater swimming. When I looked down on the water from above there was refraction, distortion, almost opacity; everything below the surface was hidden. But once my head was underneath the mask gave a most exciting clarity of vision. According to Mollie the water wasn't nearly as clear as it had been in the Mediterranean when she'd swum there, but I could make out perfectly the ribbed sand, perhaps fifteen feet below me, and the small, scattered boulders on the bottom, and the fronds of weed. I could even see fish—quite a lot of fish. They were small, and I had no idea what they were, but now that I shared their element with them I found them fascinating. They seemed so extraordinarily unconcerned as they passed in a shoal just below me.

I could have schnorkelled on the surface indefinitely, but soon Mollie said it was time to try my hand at diving. She explained the procedure with great lucidity. I must take a good lungful of air, she said, and then hold my breath. To dive, I must double myself up, push my head down, and lift up my legs—just the same, in fact, as though I'd been diving without mask and schnorkel. Once under water I must propel myself with an easy, pedalling motion of the fins, keeping my arms close to my body and using my shoulders to change direction. Arching my back, she said, would direct me upwards. I must keep enough air in my lungs to surface and to blow the water out of the schnorkel when I had surfaced. It was, she said, quite simple! I watched her go through the motions several times, and it certainly couldn't have looked easier. She dived and swam with effortless grace, and when she surfaced she squirted the water from her schnorkel in a most expert way.

I said, "Well, good-bye!—it's been nice knowing you," and tried it myself. Actually, I'd always felt completely at home in the water, and I got on pretty well. At eight or ten feet there was a slight feeling of pressure on the eardrums and eyes, and the mask felt a bit tight, but there was no real unpleasantness. The diving and swimming presented no difficulties, and the fins were an immense help. At first I was rather too aware of the equipment, too conscious of the water in the schnorkel that I'd got to blow out before I could take a breath again, but confidence grew with each dive.

We swam and dived for half an hour or more, by which time we were beginning to get a bit cold. Mollie decided we'd had enough for the moment and we went and lay in the sun for an hour. Then, when we were thoroughly warmed and rested, we packed up our clothes and equipment and made our way over the rocks to Curlew Cove.

We approached it cautiously, scanning the beach and cliffs to make sure nobody was taking any interest in us. There were some people at the other end of the beach—a man and a woman, with a small boy beside them building a sand castle—but they were a long way off and absorbed in their own affairs. There were two walkers on the clifftop, but they didn't linger. We let them pass, and then fitted on our masks and schnorkels again behind concealing rocks. Once we were out in the cove we'd probably be too far away for anyone ashore even to see we were schnorkelling.

We chose our moment, and slipped quietly off a rock into deep water and swam out to where Mollie judged *Curlew* had been anchored that morning. She admitted she wasn't very sure of the exact spot, which was hardly surprising. What we'd better do, she suggested, was start a little to seaward of where she thought the boat had been and work our way to and fro across the centre of the cove, gradually moving inwards. In that way, she said, we'd be pretty certain to pass over the anchorage, and by swimming just below the surface and looking down we ought to be able to see anything of interest on the bottom.

We tried it, but things didn't work out that way. The water around the anchorage proved to be unexpectedly deep—well over thirty feet, Mollie estimated, after an exploratory dive—and it was also less clear than in the first cove, so that we couldn't see the bottom at all. That left no alternative but hit-or-miss diving. I'd already done about all the diving I wanted to do for one morning, so after a few minutes I confined myself to patrolling the shallower water where I could just make out the sea bed, and left the hard work to Mollie. She was indefatigable. Sometimes, when there was no sign of her for over half a minute or more on end, I began to feel quite anxious, but she always reappeared quite cheerfully, blowing like a whale, anything up to twenty yards from where she'd dived. She was as competent in the water as a mermaid—and much more beautiful. All the same, she didn't get anywhere, and in the end she had to admit defeat. It would take ages, she said, to reconnoitre the cove properly when one had to keep on coming up for breath.

As we sat on the rocks afterwards, eating the ham and rolls we'd brought with us, I said, "Well, I'm very glad we came, anyway—I wouldn't have missed it for the world. From now on, you can count me a skin-diving enthusiast."

"You'll be very good with a bit more practice," she said. "All the same, the object of the exercise was to get results, you know, not just to have a pleasant swim."

"That was your idea," I said. "You'll remember I didn't expect much."

"Well, I still say the whole thing's very fishy."

This is a very fishy place."

"You're hopeless," she said. "Why won't you be serious?"

I shrugged. "What's the point? It isn't as though there's anything else we can do."

There was a little pause. Then she said, "We could get some aqualungs."

She said it very innocently, as though the notion had only just entered her head—but she was a bit too innocent. Looking at her, I hadn't a doubt that the possibility of more serious diving had been in her mind from the beginning, and that that was why she'd asked me to stay in Cornwall.

Chapter Fifteen

There wasn't really much to argue about. I'd already committed myself to the principle of the search, and going on with it was at least as sensible as starting it. As far as the office was concerned, I might just as well be hung for a sheep as a lamb. I wasn't at all sure we'd be able to get hold of aqualungs, but we could only find that out by trying—and if we could, it would be an interesting new experience. I did point out that if Thornton and Blacke *were* engaged in some nefarious business under water, by the time we'd learned to use aqualungs they'd probably have finished it and cleared off for good, but Mollie said there'd almost certainly be traces of what they'd been doing, on the sea bed. She'd practically convinced herself by now that they really had been burying the jewel case and that if we could make a thorough search at about thirty feet, we might find the place. I said that full fathom five was a pretty sinister depth, but she only smiled.

We finished our lunch and then went back to the sports shop in Falmouth for guidance. The man there told us he didn't handle aqualung equipment, which was pretty expensive and was mostly borrowed from clubs. He recommended us to go to a place called St. Treorch, not far from St. Mawes, where there was an underwater diving school run by an ex-naval man named Commander Fox who might be able to fix us up.

We drove round to St. Treorch straight away. The commander had a pleasant and—to judge by the considerable activity going on—a flourishing establishment near the water's edge, with a small salt-water swimming bath, changing huts, a shop, and a restaurant. One of his assistants pointed him out to us—a bald, burly figure in swimming trunks demonstrating something to two youths on the other side of the bath—and we went tound to have a word with him. He was showing them how to load a spring harpoon gun on land, and we stood and watched while one of them did it. The loading was accomplished satisfactorily, but as the youth raised the gun Fox said sharply, "Don't point the damn' thing at me—keep it down! Always keep it down! Now fire it off into the bath." The youth pressed the trigger and the metal harpoon went sizzling on its line into the water, where it lost its momentum after five or six feet. Fox said, "Those things can kill at fifty feet on dry land," looking at me as severely as though it had been I who'd pointed the gun at him. Then his gaze focused on Mollie, and he smiled. "Well, what can I do for you?" he said.

We introduced ourselves Mollie explained that we were working on a newspaper story that required some diving, and that we wanted to learn how to use aqualungs, at once if not sooner, and that we'd like to hire some equipment for a day or two.

He looked a bit dubious, even when we said we didn't mind how much we paid. He asked us if we'd done any skin-diving, and Mollie said, "Oh, yes! as though we'd both been at it all our lives. He asked where we proposed to dive and we said not very far from St. Treorch and close inshore, in not more than about thirty feet of water, and at that he looked relieved and said that with reasonable care we couldn't come to much harm at that depth. All the same, he couldn't accept responsibility for loaning us aqualung sets unless he was quite satisfied that we knew what we were doing, and there was a routine that couldn't be hurried beyond a certain point, and his final decision would depend entirely on how we shaped. That seemed fair enough, and we said we were ready to start right away if he was. He switched the youths to an assistant, and went off to fetch the equipment while we changed.

I'd never seen an aqualung at close quarters before? I gathered they varied a good deal, but the ones Fox brought back with him seemed, outwardly at any rate, to be remarkably simple pieces of apparatus. There were two steel alloy bottles of compressed air, which one wore strapped to the back with webbing harness. Two flexible, corrugated tubes led to a mouthpiece not very different from that of the schnorkel mouthpiece. The left tube was for breathing in, the right for breathing out. Air was supplied automatically to the diver at the correct pressure through a demand valve, and expelled through an exhaust valve. As with the schnorkel, a separate face mask covered the eyes and nose. A pressure gauge on the set showed 120 atmospheres when both bottles were full, and there was a red section marked on the gauge from 15 atmospheres downwards. The two bottles to gether, we were told, contained enough air for about eighty minutes' normal diving.

Having explained in detail how the sets worked, Fox fitted them on to us. They were pretty heavy—forty or fifty pounds—but he said that in the water we wouldn't even notice them. We spent a little time on breathing practice, and then we had to go into the swimming bath and be fitted with weight belts, so that we had what Fox called "neutral buoyancy" and neither popped to the surface nor plunged to the bottom. Afterwards we swam around for half an hour or so, getting used to the feel of the equipment under water and receiving fresh instructions from time to time as we emerged. It seemed much easier and pleasanter than schnorkelling, because breathing was natural and there was no need to bother about things like blowing water out of the tube. Fox appeared to be very pleased with out progress, but he said we'd have to come back next morning for some practice in the sea before he'd let us take the sets away. We made an appointment for early the next day, and left.

Mollie had had an idea that we ought to go along to the cove at low tide that evening and see if *Curlew* was there again, but the hour had already passed and in any case we were both worn out after the day's exertions. When I rang the office after dinner I was almost too tired to care what they said—but as it happened they didn't say anything. Hatcher was having his day off, Blair had gone home early because there was no news about, and Ridley, who was holding the fort, couldn't have cared less whether I reported back or not. I said vaguely that something had happened and that I wouldn't be in in the morning and would be ringing again, and that was that. I went to bed at nine-thirty, and in ten minutes I was dead to the world.

We breakfasted early the next day and then drove straight back to St. Treorch. The commander was ready for us. This time we had to fit on our own sets under his watchful eye. I thought we'd finished with the schnorkels, but it seemed we had to carry them in our belts, in case they should be needed some time for emergency surfacing. When he was quite satisfied, he took us down to a private cove and the three of us went into the sea together from a convenient rock.

Once in, we were three independent people, with almost no sense of hearing, and no means of communication except by sign or touch. The masks made it difficult even to judge the expression of a face. I felt some slight qualms at first, a rather disconcerting sense of remoteness, but the feeling soon passed as I concentrated on the job. I tried to remember all the things that Fox had said about breathing, and to aim at an even, steady rhythm, and soon got into the way of it. I thought again how much pleasanter aqualunging was than schnorkelling. Swimming was almost effortless, and I found myself manoeuvring with astonishing ease. When I first went down to fifteen feet or so I felt a slight pain in my ears, as Fox had warned I might, but it passed when I swallowed and I didn't get it again.

We stayed in long enough to use up a whole bottle of air, and then the commander motioned us out. He asked us how we felt, and we both said "Fine!" He gave a satisfied nod. Then he proceeded to give us a lot more advice. If we *did* go down deep, he said, all sorts of horrible things could happen to us, so we'd better watch our depth meter carefully. Again, if we over-exerted ourselves, we could get carbon dioxide poisoning and what was called "shallow water blackout," because under water you couldn't pant and get rid of the poison that way as you could on land, so we must remember to take it easy all the time. We should always dive slowly, he reminded us, and come up even more slowly, not more than twenty-five feet a minute. Finally he emphasised once more a point he'd made before we'd gone into the sea—that we should never forcibly retain a full breath from the apparatus when surfacing because if we did we could damage our lungs even from a depth of seven or eight feet. And of course, he added, we should never dive alone, or lose sight of our companion, or stay in the water after we'd begun to feel cold.

I thought he'd finished then, but back at the swimming bath he gave us some more instruction. We had to practise switching from aqualung mouthpiece to schnorkel mouthpiece under water, which was quite tricky; and he also showed us how to surface and clear the mask and tubes of water in case they got flooded through a leak, or the mask accidentally coming off. Finally he recharged our bottles with a powerful air compressor he kept for the purpose, and said he'd be seeing us, and wished us luck. We were on our own!

We packed the gear away in the car, and discussed plans. Obviously we didn't want to use up our air on more practising, and in any case it seemed wiser to rest and conserve our resources. It was already almost lunch-time, and in the afternoon the tide would be high and we'd have too much depth to contend with. The best time to make our reconnaissance, we decided, was a couple of hours before low water. Conditions would be good, and in the event of *Curlew* turning up again we'd be well out of the way before she arrived.

We had a leisurely lunch at Falmouth, and in the afternoon we took the now familir route round the Helford river and parked the car by the barley field. Then we humped the diving gear to the cove, each set wrapped in a car rug in case we met anyone on the way. As an additional precaution, we kept close to the dry stone wall as we walked along the clifftop. We examined the cove carefully from above, and when we'd made sure the coast was clear we dropped down and settled ourselves in a quiet place among the boulders.

As the tide slowly fell, exposing the weedy rocks, our sense of excitement grew. In my case, it was the thought of diving on our own rather than any belief that we should find anything which quickened my pulse. I made an effort to calm down, because Fox had emphasised that a relaxed frame of mind was essential for good diving, but I could scarcely wait. We'd fixed on five o'clock as the time to start putting on our equipment, and we set to work on the dot. But we'd hardly unwrapped the gear when two men and a girl came down to the cove and began larking about on the beach, and we had to wait for more than half an hour before they moved on. Then, keeping well back in the shelter of the rocks, we went conscientiously through the drill—cleaning and fitting the masks, testing the masks, testing the aqualungs in a pool for leaks, and making sure the harness was secure. Just before six, we lowered ourselves gently into the water.

Once I was in, and swimming, my nervousness soon passed. My aqualung was working perfectly, and by the time we were well out in the cove I'd almost forgotten I was wearing it. We surfaced and had a good look round, checking our position from shore rocks that we'd noted the previous day as being more or less in line with the anchorage. Then we dived again. The depth meter showed twenty-three feet at the bottom, which was fine.

Our plan of campaign was the same as on the first occasion—to swim to and fro across the centre of the cove, starting a little to the seaward side of where we thought *Curlew* had been, and gradually moving inwards. This time, though, we could keep close to the bottom all the way. The sea bed was sandy, with nothing to obstruct the view. The water was quite clear enough for our purpose. If we found nothing else, at least we ought to be able to find the holes left by Curlew's anchor without much trouble.

We swam along about six feet apart, slowly and easily. The water seemed warmer than it had been the day before. The bubbles from our exhaust valves streamed up reassuringly above us. At intervals of a few yards we stopped and scraped up handfuls of sand, marking our route, so that we shouldn't cover the same stretch twice. When my depth meter showed that we were getting too near the side of the cove, we turned and swam back the other way on a slightly different track.

We did five trips without seeing anything more exciting than fish. On the sixth, Mollie suddenly swam close and pointed to a dark, box-like object over on her right and we put on speed and investigated—but it was only an old biscuit tin that had been thrown overboard from a boat. We continued on our course, and turned again. By now we were in a mere fifteen feet of water, and clearly much closer inshore than *Curlew* had been. I looked at Mollie, and her eyelids and eyebrows went up in a kind of optical shrug.

At the next turn we abandoned the shallow water and swam out until we were well to seaward of our starting point, with a depth of nearly thirty-five feet. We set off across the cove again. Almost at once we spotted an unmistakable mark—an anchor mark. We swam on a few yards—and then, slowly, unbelievably, some large object took shape ahead of us. Mollie saw it at the same moment as I did, and we kicked out hard and reached it together.

It was a sunken boat—quite a biggish boat. And the name on the stern was *Mary Ann*.

Chapter Sixteen

So Thornton and Blake *had* been concerned in the raid—and Mollie had pulled it off again! I moved close to her and gave her arm a congratulatory squeeze, the peak expression of underwater emotion. Then I slowly circled the boat. There was no question of thinking anything out at that stage; all I wanted to do was look.

Mary Ann was listed over towards her port side, at quite a gentle angle, her shallow keel resting on firm sand. She was completely motionless in the deep, still water. She was anchored fore and aft, and judging by the absence of drag marks the anchors had been laid out by the divers after she'd sunk.

With Mollie beside me, I swam up over the cockpit and approached the cabin doors, which were shut. The lock, I discovered, was broken, and dents in the woodwork around it showed that it had been forced. I fastened the doors back against the cabin bulkhead, and we both peered inside. Light was entering not only through the portholes but through the roof, several planks of which had been broken out with some violence. The whole interior of the cabin was in a state of wild disorder. All the floor boards on the starboard side had been taken up, and were jammed or floating against the deckhead above the port berth, with a lot of other debris. The starboard berth had been practically dismantled, so that the ribs and planks of the hull were exposed both above and below the water line. A short-handled axe, which had evidently been used used for the demolition, lay in the bottom of the ship. Most of the work must have been done, I thought, while she'd still floated, for the exertion under water would have been terrific.

My eyes were growing more accustomed now to the dim light,

and as I gazed around the cabin, trying to memorise every detail for the descriptive piece I should soon be writing, my attention was caught by some small, irregularly spaced holes with splintered edges, just below the water line in the starboard side of the ship. There were six of them, and the angle of all of them was downwards. I followed the line of them, and saw that there were more holes, this time in the bottom of the boat. There wasn't much doubt that shots had been fired through the hull from the outside. A moment later I noticed a small metal object protruding from the base of the fixed cabin table—the flattened remains of a bullet. There wasn't any doubt.

We moved cautiously into the cabin. Just beyond the table there was something that looked like an open attaché-case lying bottom upwards across the ribs of the boat, and as I drew nearer I saw that it was the lizard skin jewel case that had been stolen from *Wanderer*. Then I caught the sheen of metal again, and picked up a jewelled ring from the silt in the bilge. I started to search around for more pieces, and so did Mollie. Almost at once the water in the cabin began to lose its transparency as our movements stirred up the sediment in the bottom of the boat, and soon it was so opaque that we couldn't see a thing and there seemed no point in staying any longer. We fumbled our way to the door and swam out of the cockpit and round the side of the ship and had a look at the bullet holes from the outside. They must have been made, I decided, by bullets of pretty high calibre, fired at very close range, for the hull was stout.

I glanced at my aqualung pressure gauge, and it showed seventy atmospheres. I still had a whole bottle of air, and Mollie presumably had the same. But there was nothing more to hang about for—obviously the thing now was to report to Anstey as soon as possible. I indicated to Mollie that we should start for the shore, and she nodded. We turned away from the boat and began to swim slowly along the sandy bottom towards the beach, judging our direction by the change in the depth meter We were making good progress in about twenty feet when, looking ahead, I suddenly saw a figure moving thtough the water. It was a man, aqualunged, and he was swimming straight towards us. Just behind him was another man. Thornton and Blake had come back!

And that wasn't all. Both men were carrying loaded harpoon guns, and pointing them at us in a most business like way. With a shock of horror I realised that this wasn't just a chance encounter—that they hadn't dived to carry on with their work on the boat, and happened to meet us. They'd come to hunt us! They must have seen our bubbles, and guessed that we were snooping about round the boat, and dived to intercept us. With one murder on their hands already, they'd nothing to lose by two more—and now that we knew so much, they couldn't afford to let us escape. They'd come—to kill us. This story, which had been all theory until our discovery of *Mary Ann*, which until a few moments ago I'd treated almost flippantly, had suddenly become an affair of life and death for us.

Mollie had stopped swimming and was staring at me. I gripped her arm and swung her round, and we swam away together, away from the guns, faster than we'd ever swum before under water. It was dangerous, I knew, but even shallow-water blackout would be no worse than a harpoon in the small of the back. After a few seconds I turned to see how we were doing. I thought we were all right. It was difficult to judge distance accurately under water, but the leading man was certainly fifteen feet away, and that was well out of effective range. The trouble was that by now we'd lost our sense of direction. I looked at the depth meter and it showed nearly thirty feet. Safety lay among the tangle of rocks near the shore, but we were swimming out to sea. I swung to the right, making sure that Mollie was keeping close to me, and looked back again. They were overhauling us! Thornton, brown-skinned and lean, was in the lead and coming up fast. They were probably much more expert at this underwater business than we were. They were going to catch us! Already my breathing was erratic, my heart was pounding—I couldn't possibly keep up the pace. The distance now looked more like ten feet, and both men were holding their guns forward at the ready, their fingers on the triggers.

The under-water light was growing brighter—we were moving

into the shallows. But not quickly enough. They were still closing in. Perhaps, I thought, I ought to turn and try to grapple with Thornton before he could shoot—anything was better than being spitted from behind. Or perhaps if we surfaced it would be more difficult for them to shoot? I didn't know . . . Then, a few yards to the right, I saw under-water rocks and steered Mollie towards them with a touch on her arm. A tall slab of granite offered cover, and Mollie glided behind it and I followed her round, my spine tingling. Then we stopped. There was rock all round us, and no way out. We'd swum into some sort of underwater grotto.

I turned in despair, certain that this was the end. But it wasn't. The gap on either side of the rock slab was so narrow, I now saw, that it would be impossible for our pursuers to shoot into the grotto. The angles were all wrong for their long guns. We were in a trap, but as long as we stayed there they couldn't harpoon us. They must come in after us, or wait—and if they came in, we'd be on equal terms. Their diving equipment would be as vulnerable in an underwater tussle as ours. We disposed ourselves so that one of us was on guard on each side of the slab. Suddenly, a head appeared, only a few inches away from me. I thrust out a hand and tore at the face mask. My fingers clawed down the glass, but I couldn't get a grip, and the head disappeared. I'd missed my chance. But I doubted if they'd try to come in again—and they didn't. When, after a moment or two, nothing else happened, I peered out very cautiously myself and saw that they were resting motionless in the water a dozen feet away, like two watchful fish.

I took a quick look round our sanctuary. It was not so much a grotto, I saw, as a wedge-shaped cleft in the rocks, just wide enough to hold the two of us without jostling. Above our heads there was a gap in the roof, too narrow to squeeze through, but admitting a fair amount of light. The water above the gap must be very shallow, I thought—and the depth meter confirmed that. From the sandy floor on which we stood, it registered a mere eight feet. If we'd only had a few more seconds to spare, we'd have got safely ashore.

Several minutes passed. I half expected that one of the men

would try to attack us from above, pushing his gun through the gap—but neither of them did. Either the existence of the gap hadn't occurred to them, or they were content to wait. They could certainly afford to wait. They had started their dive long after we had—they would have air long after ours was exhausted. I glanced at my pressure gauge, and it showed only twenty-five atmospheres—enough for about a quarter of an hour. I looked at Mollie's and hers showed nearly thirty. She'd probably taken the sudden crisis more coolly, and had therefore breathed less air. I wasn't surprised.

I tried hard to think of something effective to do, but I couldn't. Being under water, I found, didn't make consecutive thought any easier. I longed to be able to discuss the situation with Mollie, but there wasn't any means of communication. It was ghastly not being able to talk. With the masks virtually hiding all expression, there wasn't even much comfort in proximity. Indeed, there was no comfort at all. The water had seemed warm enough when we'd first entered it, but we'd been immersed for over an hour and the effect was numbing. Not that that mattered much, when we'd only air left for a few minutes anyway.

I looked out again. The two men were still there in the same place, and their guns were still held at the ready. There didn't seem to be much hope of a successful break-out. Yet if the choice was between slow, gasping suffocation and trying for a break, we'd obviously have to try. There was always the possibility that they might miss with the harpoons, or at least that we'd escape with minor wounds. Once in the open, we'd need only a few strokes to reach the shore, and if we weren't too crippled we might still make it. I looked at my pressure gauge again. The needle was already well into the red sector, which meant I'd less than fifteen atmospheres left—and I remembered Fox had warned us that breathing would begin to grow difficult when there was still quite a bit of air in the bottles. A matter of minutes now!—and then any action would be too late. If we were going to try for a break, we must do it right away. I showed the gauge to Mollie and made urgent gestures, hoping she'd understand—pointing to the opening beside me, making swimming movements, pointing in the direction of the shore. She gave a slow nod. I took one of her hands in both of mine and held it for a moment—a wretchedly inadequate farewell. Then I moved to the opening.

I was just going to stick my head out when she clutched my shoulder and drew me back. She pointed to her depth meter, then to the gap in the rock over our heads, then to the schnorkel in her belt. I looked at my meter, and saw that the depth had dropped by a foot since we'd swum into the grotto. Water still covered the gap, but it was gently swirling water, with a littl foam in it. Not very far up, there was air. The question was, how far?

I hesitated, but only for a second. It was a gamble, with death as the almost certain penalty of failure—but it seemed to offer more hope than a break-out. I mentally rehearsed the transfer drill that Fox had taught us, and I found I remembered it quite clearly. I drew my schnorkel from my belt, took a full breath of air from the aqualung, and held it while I removed the mouth-piece. Then I thrust the schnorkel mouthpiece into my mouth instead. Water filled the schnorkel and ran into my mouth, but I kept it there harmlessly, still holding my breath. Then I got my face as near to the gap as I could and pushed the schnorkel up and blew the water out of my mouth and out of the tube with a long, lung-emptying breath. *Now!*

I breathed in—and air came through the tube, not water. I was reprieved.

It was Mollie's turn, now. I felt pretty bad as I watched her, though I felt sure she could do it. She'd managed it in the swimming bath without any trouble. The tricky moment was the moment of transfer—if she lost her air, then, she wouldn't be able to blow out the tube. And there was nothing at all I could do to help her. But I needn't have worried—she accomplished it perfectly. A second or two later-she was breathing steadily through her tube beside me.

For the moment we were safe, but I still couldn't feel any real hope. We'd postponed the end, but that was about all. Thornton and Blake wouldn't stay out there immobile for ever. Before long they'd decide that we must be dead, and they'd probably come in to make sure we were, and then we'd be entirely at their mercy. Or they might look around first, they might surface and catch sight of the protruding schnorkels and drag them from our mouths. It could happen any second—and it wasn't a nice thought. The mere idea made breathing more difficult. Better not to think!

I had almost no notion now of the passing of time. Earlier the aqualung pressure gauge had given us a rough indication, but now there was nothing. I knew that dusk couldn't be far away, for the light that came through to the grotto was growing dim. I felt terribly cold. We were clinging to life with our teeth, literally, but we wouldn't be able to cling much longer. The cold would get us. It seemed extraordinary that Thornton and Blake hadn't come in yet. Their own air supply must be nearing its end by now, even supposing their bottles had been quite full to start with. I couldn't understand what they were up to at all. They must know that our bottles would be exhausted by this time.

Suddenly I drew water in through my schnorkel as a wavelet washed over the top of it. I managed to blow it out, but a moment later the same thing happened again. The tide had obviously turned and was rising once more. Mollie was having trouble too.

Now we'd *have* to run the gaunlet of the harpoons—and one single lungful of air! I touched Mollie's arm, and pointed to the entrance. She understood, and nodded. There was no time to lose. I indicated that I'd go first. I filled my lungs through the sehnorkel, and held my breath, and moved to the opening of the grotto. I peered out cautiously. I couldn't see anyone. The two men were no longer where they had been. I swam out and looked around. There was no one about at all. With bursting lungs I surfaced, and pushed up my face mask and took a deep gulp of air. It felt wonderful to be able to breathe freely again. I slipped off the aqualung and held it, buoying myself up with it. There still wasn't anyone around. A moment later, Mollie shot up beside me.

We'd made it!

Together we swam to the shore and clambered out on to a rock. Neither of us had much to say—we were too exhausted, too cold, too unutterably relieved to talk. Mollie pulled off her swimming cap and stretched out flat, with a long, shuddering sigh. "God, that was awful!" she murmured. Her face was drawn with fatigue; her fingers and toes were white and bloodless. I was in scarcely better shape myself. But the air felt almost tropically warm after the water, and we soon began to revive. Presently I sat up and began to chafe Mollie's hands and feet, and that warmed me, too. After I'd rubbed and slapped for several minutes I said, "I think we ought to dress now," and she nodded.

I was just going to get to my feet when, from somewhere very close by, a voice said sharply, "Don't move!" and a man appeared from behind a rock with a gun in his hand.

It was Guy Mellor!

Chapter Seventeen

There was a short, tense silence. Then Mollie said, "So you are in it!"

"Oh, yes, I'm in it," Mellor said. "You had the right idea in the first place, but you gave up too soon." He took a step towards us and sat down on a rock just out of reach. His pose was so nonchalant, his attitude so unaggressive, that no one looking at us would have supposed for a moment that anything was wrong. But he kept the gun pointing at us, and his eyes were watchful.

"In case you're thinking of starting a rough house," he said to me, "don't! This thing would go off at once."

I didn't doubt it. If he'd conspired with the others, and murder had resulted, he hadn't much to lose, either. In any case, I'd never felt less like tackling a man with a gun than I did at that moment.

I said, "Do you mind if we get our clothes—they're not far away."

He hesitated. "Better wait a bit."

"We'll probably get pneumonia," Mollie said.

"That's the least thing you've got to worry about!"

I said, "What are we waiting for, anyway?"

"*I'm* waiting for reinforcements. You're waiting because I'm waiting."

I glanced around the cove. Dusk was falling quickly, now. The beach was deserted, and as far as I could make out, so was the clifftop. I looked across at *Curlew*, anchored out in the cove. There didn't seem to be anyone aboard her. A moment later, though, her dinghy nosed out from behind her bows, with Thornton and Blake in it. They were fully dressed now, even to yachting caps. Blake was rowing. They came slowly in towards the beach.

I said, "What baffles me is why your murdering friends didn't stay underwater long enough to make sure they'd finished the job."

"Well, I can answer that for you," Mellor said easily. "They had to conserve their air—they've a bit more work to do on the boat. So they left me to take charge of you."

"How did they know we were down there—was it the bubbles?"

"As a matter of fact, it was me—I was around when they came in, and I gave them a situation report."

"I suppose you've been watching us all the time?"

"Naturally—you, and the cove. You did rather give yourselves away, didn't you? Particularly Miss Bourne." He gave Mollie a faint grin. Even with the gun in his lap, he still managed to look debonair. "Your attention was very flattering—too flattering!"

I said, "So you just sat here and waited until we came up."

"That's about it. Though frankly, I didn't think you would come up. I thought you'd had it."

"That didn't mean a thing to you of course."

He shrugged. "It's not that we bear you any malice, old chap, don't think that, but you did not us in a bit of a bit of a spot, didn't you? Once you'd found the boat, what could we do?"

I said, "Who shot the holes in her—Scott?"

"Who else?"

"And who killed Scott?"

"You know," he said, "I'd have thought you'd have learned the dangers of curiosity by now."

"You don't imagine you'll get away with this, do you?"

"Why not?—we practically have."

Mollie said, "That's what you think."

By now, Thornton and Blake had beached their dinghy and were strolling slowly along the sand towards us. The calm, leisurely way in which everyone was behaving was enough to send a chill down the spine. They seemed so sure of themselves. Thornton even stopped once to gaze down into a pool as he picked his way over a pile of rocks. They might have been any couple of yachtsmen taking a pleasant constitutional ashore before supper. That, no doubt, was the idea.

When they reached us, they also sat down. Thornton had a gun, too. I'd never really studied him before, but now I did, and I didn't at all like what I saw. His affability at our first meeting had been the thinnest of veneers. He had very cold, light blue eyes, and a tight, ugly mouth that turned down at the corners. It was a tough face, empty of pity. He gave us barely a glance.

Mellor said, "Well, here they are—they walked straight into my arms. What are we going to do with them?"

"We'll take them along to the boat," Thornton said. His tone was authoritative—there was no doubt that he was the boss. Blake, by comparison, seemed a nonentity. Unlike Mellor and Thornton, Blake was looking, I thought, a bit unhappy about things.

Mollie said, "We'll need our clothes."

Thornton gazed along the beach, as though considering whether it was dark enough to start moving. Then he got to his feet. "All right, we'll pick them up on the way. Tony, you bring the gear."

Blake hoisted our two aqualungs on to his shoulders. Mellor said, "Okay, Curtis, get cracking—I'm right behind you."

I set off towards the rocks where we'd left our things. Mollie walked beside me. We had a bit of a job finding the clothes in the failing light, but a gleam of white brought us to them in the end. Thornton took charge of Mollie. He stood watching her from the top of a rock while she dressed, but I doubted if he had a thought in his mind but jewels. I gave myself a vigorous towelling and got gratefully into my clothes. I left my swimming shorts lying in the sand, in the desperate hope that someone would find them and do something about it, but Mellor noticed them and made me pick them up. "It's no good, old chap," he said, "we don't miss a trick."

In a few moments, Mollie returned with Thornton and we all moved down to the dinghy. At the water's edge, Thornton said, "You do understand, don't you, that if there's any nonsense you'll both be shot out of hand!" He watched while Mellor pushed the dinghy out. Then he told me to get in and take the oars. Mollie was placed in the bows. Mellor and Thornton sat facing us on the stern seat, their guns ready. Blake pushed us off, and I began to row. It seemed hopeless to try anything. The dinghy was a beamy boat and I didn't think it would upset easily. In any case, we'd probably be dead before we reached the water. I kept rowing, and in a few moments we were alongside *Curlew*. Thornton ordered me up the short ladder and followed me into the cockpit. Mellor came aboard behind Mollie. Mellor stayed with us while Thornton took the dinghy back for Blake and the gear. They were an efficient team.

It was almost dark now, and I couldn't see much in the cockpit, but I made a mental note of its lay-out. It was pretty wide, eight or nine feet, with a square stern. There was a seat on each side, from the counter to the saloon bulkhead, with lockers underneath, and there were more lockers in the stern. The engine was housed under a wooden casing about five feet from the saloon door. The wheel and controls were on the port side of the door.

That was about all I had time to notice before Thornton and Blake returned. One of them switched on the saloon light, and we were taken inside. The saloon was spacious, but that was about all that could be said for it. There was a sleeping berth on each side of it, a table in the middle, and a small galley compartment near the door—and not much else. *Curlew* was certainly no luxury boat. The paint on the walls was dirty and peeling, and everything looked in a pretty scruffy state. No attempt had been made to keep the place tidy. The wet aqualungs and harpoon guns, I noticed, had been thrown down on one of the bunks and had soaked the cover. Obviously, no one cared.

While Mellor stood guard, Thornton went through my pockets. He took away a knife, which was the only thing I could conceivably have used as a weapon. Afterwards he ran quickly through the contents of Mollie's handbag. Then we were taken through another door into a small forecabin, with two more bunks along its converging sides.

"Your stateroom!" Mellor said. He looked carefully around as though satisfying himself there was nothing lying about that we could make trouble with. He needn't have bothered—the forecabin was even barer than the saloon.

I said, "What's the programme, Mellor?"

He shrugged. "Don't ask me—Thornton runs the show."

"Well, do you suppose we could have a drink and something to eat? We've had a pretty gruelling time, you know."

"I'll see," he said, and went out, locking the cabin door behind him.

An electric bulb above our heads gave out a dim light, and Mollie took a mirror from her bag and began tidying her hair and making up her face.

"How do you feel?" I said.

She gave me a wry look. "Fairly pessimistic, at the moment."

"Are you warm now?"

"Oh, yes, I'm warm enough."

"Well, we're still alive—which is more than I expected to be a little while ago."

"Me, too," she said. "Let's hope it lasts!"

While she was busy with the mirror I had a look round our quarters. There was a porthole above each bunk—far too small to get through, of course. There were lockers under the beds, both of them empty. For'ard of the cabin, there was another small door leading to a toilet compartment in the forepeak. I had a sudden hope that there might be a hatch in the roof there, but there wasn't. I came out again, and inspected the cabin door. It was lightly constructed and the lock didn't look very strong. I could probably break it open if I wanted to. But with all that armament outside, there wasn't any point.

Presently the key turned in the lock and Mellor came in again. He was carrying two sizeable tots of whisky, some biscuits, and a lump of cheese. Blake was covering him from behind with the gun. Mellor said, "I'm afraid you'll have to eat in the dark—Thornton's orders. We can't risk any signalling." He took the bulb from the cabin light and went out, re-locking the door behind him.

The whisky went down wonderfully. So did the food. Afterwards I gave Mollie a cigarette and lit my pipe and we lay down on the bunks.

"Well, they've treated us pretty well so far," I said.

"Oh, yes, apart from hunting us with harpoons! What do you suppose they're going to do—stay anchored here all night?"

"It looks like it," I said. "They've turned on the riding light—I can see its reflection in the water."

She was silent for a moment or two. Then she said, "I'm sorry I let you in for this, Hugh."

"Nonsense! I'm of age, aren't I?"

"It's going to be a terrific story if we ever have the chance to write it."

"Yes," I said, without much conviction.

I lay still for a while, listening to the murmur of voices from the cockpit. I wished I could hear what they were saying, but nothing came through clearly. Once I caught the chink of crockery—they were probably having their supper, too. Presently there was a shuffling of feet, and a sound like someone getting into the dinghy. I looked out through the porthole. It was a wonderful night, clear and starlit and very warm. The curve of the hull hid the stern from view, but after a moment the dinghy came into sight. There was one man in it, rowing for the shore. I thought it was Mellor, but I wasn't sure. The voices in the cockpit continued to rumble away.

Mollie was very quiet. I leaned across, and saw that she'd dropped off to sleep. I wasn't surprised. I stretched out on the bunk again, and thought about the extraordinary mess we'd got into. It was difficult to be at all hopeful. Thornton and Mellor were obviously quite ruthless. Blake would follow his leader. We were completely in their power, and there didn't seem to be a single thing we could do . . . Not at the moment, anyway.

My thoughts switched to the raid, and for a while I occupied myself in trying to piece together the bits of information that we now had. But I soon gave it up. There seemed no point in milling over a situation that was only half understood, particularly when our own prospects were so dubious. Better to follow Mollie's example, and recoup lost energies. I relaxed, and very soon I was asleep, too.

Chapter Eighteen

I was wakened by a loud bump, and sat up in alarm. I'd been dead to the world, and in the darkness it took me a moment or two to remember where I was. Then I saw Mollie's face, faintly lit by the glow of a cigarette, and everything came back. She was sitting at the foot of my bunk, beside the open port.

"Hallo," I said. "Have you been awake long?"

"Not long . . ."

"What was that noise?"

"Only the dinghy coming back—it banged against the hull . . . Hugh, there were *two* men in it."

"Two? Are you sure?"

"Certain."

"Then that makes four of them altogether."

"Yes."

"It's getting to be quite a gang," I said ruefully. "Not that one more makes much difference at this stage . . . I wonder who he is, though."

"He was just a dark shape in the stern to me."

"Well, we'll know soon . . . Any idea of the time?"

Mollie drew on her cigarette and held the glowing tip close to her watch. "Ten minutes to midnight."

"Heavens, we've slept for nearly three hours. I must say I feel better for it, too."

"So do I . . . Listen!"

The outer door from the cockpit had opened. A voice—Thornton's—said, "We might just as well make ourselves comfortable."

"They'll hear everything if we talk in there." That was Blake.

"Does it matter?" Thornton said.

They came in, with a lot of foot-shuffling. Berth springs creaked as someone sat down heavily. They seemed to be arranging themselves round the saloon table. I heard Mellor say sharply, "Mind that diving kit, Tony." The shuffling continued as they settled down. Then a new voice said, "Well—this is a damn' fine mess you've got us into."

For a moment I could scarcely believe my ears. Perhaps I didn't want to believe them, because. I'd liked the man and privately given him a clean bill. But there couldn't be any doubt about it—I'd heard that West Country burr too often lately to make any mistake. The newcomer was Harris, the captain of *Wanderer*.

Mollie had recognised him, too. I felt her hand close tightly on my arm, signalling the fact. We listened, hardly daring to breathe in case we missed anything.

Thornton said, with a touch of asperity, "It could be a much worse mess."

"Could it?"

"Of course it could. If they'd got away, we'd all be on the run by now."

"Well, we can't keep them locked up for ever," Harris said, "so what difference does it make? We'll be on the run soon enough."

There was a little silence. I think it was the most eloquent silence I'd ever known. I hadn't much doubt what was coming next—and I was right.

"We'll have to do something about them, that's all," Thornton said. The matter-of-factness of his tone made my blood run cold.

Harris said slowly, "You know I'll never agree to that."

"You don't have to concern yourself about it," Thornton said. "We can easily manage it between us if you're squeamish."

"You ought to have been a bloody butcher!" Harris broke out with sudden violence.

"Easy!" Mellor said. "We're all friends here!"

"If it comes to butchery," Thornton said, "we've all of us done a bit of it in our time. Knives in the back, too!—but maybe you've forgotten, Harris."

"That was war—it was quite different . . . What you're suggesting turns my stomach. My God, I wish I'd never met you."

"It's a bit late to think about that, now."

"I ought to have known you couldn't be trusted."

"If you're still harping on the Scott episode," Thornton said coldly, "I told you before, I had no choice. If he'd been allowed to go on shooting, we'd probably never have got the boat away at all. Anyway, I only meant to wing him—it was just bad luck the bullet got him in the head."

"We agreed the guns weren't to be loaded," Harris said.

"Well, it's a good thing they were, that's all I can say. If they hadn't been, we'd all have been finished. And don't imagine you'll be able to wriggle out of your share of the business, because nobody's ever going to believe you didn't know the guns were loaded. You're in this thing up to the neck—literally!"

"Maybe I am," Harris said, "but I'm not getting in any deeper—and I mean that. There's going to be no more killing."

Thornton gave an impatient exclamation. "Look, Harris, face the facts, will you? If those two tell their story, we're sunk. You know that as well as I do. If they don't, we're all right. No one else knows a thing. So what is there to argue about? There won't be any hitches, I assure you. Tony and I will do one more dive in the morning, and by then we'll have recovered practically all the stuff. Afterwards, we'll take the boat out and get rid of those two—if we drop them into deep water with plenty of ballast they'll never be heard of again. You won't even need to be around—you can go back to *Wanderer* to-night and carry on just as before. I only asked you to come over so that I could bring you up to date. Guy will stay on for the dive, and that'll be all we'll need of him, too. He can pack up his tent and get back to town. I'll see the stuff reaches Amsterdam, and we'll divide up as we arranged. Everything will work out fine."

"We hope!" Mellor said.

"Anyway," Thornton added, "there's simply no alternative."

"That's just it, there is," Harris said. "We don't have to kill them.

Why can't we just tie them up and leave them somewhere? There's a cave back there on the beach—it's just the place. And then . . ." His voice dropped to a low murmur, so that I couldn't hear what he was saying any more.

There was a pause. Then Thornton said, in his normal voice, "And after that, what? Suppose we did take this tub to Eire and scuttle her off the coast and go ashore, how long do you suppose we'd stay free? The police would have our descriptions flashed over there the moment those two got loose. We wouldn't have a chance."

A fist crashed down on the table. "Do you have to shout everything from the housetops, you bloody fool? If you tell them everything we're planning to do, of course we haven't a chance."

"It's you that's the fool, Harris," Thornton said. "Do you imagine the police wouldn't think of Eire, anyway?"

"It doesn't mean they'd get us, even so. We could find jobs, change our names, maybe go to sea . . ."

"That's a far cry from having a boatyard of your own," Thornton scoffed.

"It's better than more murders."

"Well, I certainly don't mean to go to sea," Thornton said. "I want to enjoy what we've worked for, in comfort—and I intend to. What about you, Guy?"

"I'm with you," Mellor said. "I don't think we'd have one chance in a hundred. In fact, I doubt if this old tore-out would even make Eire."

"Tony?"

There was a little silence. Then Blake said, "I don't like it, John, but I suppose you're right."

"That's settled, then," Thornton said. "Now, let's have a drink."

"Wait a minute!" Harris's voice had its own note of authority. "You three think you can do as you like, don't you?—but you're wrong. You think because I'm always being pushed around, you can push me around, too. Well, you'd better think again."

"It's a majority decision, Harris."

"To hell with that. Now you listen to me. I came in with you on this thing because I wanted some dough, and the way the Attwoods were flinging theirs around. I didn't see why they shouldn't lose a little. It was a tough job, a risk, but it seemed a risk worth taking. There was even a bit of adventure about it. But I never countenanced murder, and I never would. It's not my line. I don't mind telling you when I found Scott lying there dead I was tempted to spill the whole story right away."

"And spend the rest of your life in jail?" Thornton said. "I'm not surprised you resisted the temptation!"

"Okay—I didn't do it. Maybe I hadn't got the guts. It was all finished, anyway—the man was dead and I couldn't alter it. But this isn't finished—it's just going to begin. And I'm not having it. Is that clear, Thornton?—I'm not having it."

Thornton said, "I wouldn't say it was clear, no. What exactly are you going to do about it?"

"I'm going to stay here to see that nothing happens to those two. In the morning, we'll dump them ashore, and then we'll take our chance. That's my last word."

There was a tense silence. Then, very softly, Thornton said, "You know, Harris, I think it may be!"

Blake said, in an anxious voice, "Easy, John, we've got enough on our hands . . ." Then silence fell again.

It was unbearable not to be able to see what was going on. I tried to look through the keyhole, but the key blocked the view. Then I noticed that there was a tiny gleam of light coming through the top of the door where it didn't fit very well, and I piled some cushions on the floor and stood on them and managed to get my eye to the crack.

There was quite a tableau in the saloon.

Thornton and Harris, seated near the outer door, faced each other across the table like duellists—except that only Thornton had a gun. He was pointing it at Harris's chest. Harris, his big brown hands clutching the edge of the table, was watching him, motionless. Blake was watching him, too. Mellor was watching Harris.

Mellor said, "You might just as well string along with us, Harris.

There aren't any boatyards in heaven, you know."

Harris said nothing.

Then in a fraction of a second, the situation exploded in chaos. Harris ducked and made a grab under the table. He must have got hold of Thornton's foot, because Thornton was dragged off his seat before he could shoot. Mellor hurled himself on Harris. The table collapsed with a sound of rending wood. Blake seemed to be tangled up in the wreckage. Suddenly Harris tore himself away from Mellor and reached for the light switch and plunged the cabin into darkness.

It was a free-for-all, now—and an opportunity such as I hadn't dared to hope for. I stepped back and crashed my foot against the lock of the cabin door. The lock broke, the door burst open, and I waded in. A pale face rose in front of me and I hit it hard and it merged again with the darkness. I couldn't see much but I could hear plenty—there were grunts and gasps from all sides. Then someone got the cockpit door open and a figure was outlined for a moment against the stars. At once there was a flash, and a deafening report. The figure stumbled, recovered, and fell. Someone switched on the light again. I snatched up a bit of the broken table and struck at the light bulb but missed it. Thornton, struggling up out of of the debris, turned his gun on me.

"All right," he said, "keep still, everbody. The fight's over." He got slowly to his feet.

By now Mellor had pulled out his own gun and was covering me, too. Blood trickled down his face from a cut over his eye. Blake was nursing his jaw. After a moment, Thornton went out into the cockpit and bent over Harris.

"How is he?" Mellor called, and waited. We all waited.

"He's dead," Thornton said. "He won't bother us any more."

Mollie, just behind me, gave a little gasp. Blake said, "The fool!—oh, the damn' fool!"

Mellor jerked his gun towards us. "What about these two?"

"They'll keep—there's enough mess already. Get them back in the cabin."

"In you go!" Mellor said.

I followed Mollie in, and shut the door. The lock didn't work any more, but the latch still did, after a fashion. The panel above it had split from the force of my blow, and now Mollie was able to look through the door, too. We watched while the survivors tidied up.

Blake stayed in the saloon, gathering up the bits of mahogany that had once been a table and stacking them on one of the berths. He'd got Mellor's gum; and he kept glancing towards our door. His nerve didn't seem too good, and I thought he was much too trigger-happy to take any chances with. We kept very still, and watched Thornton and Mellor out in the cockpit. We couldn't see everything, but we could see enough. Mellor had got a tarpaulin from somewhere and was spreading it out on the cockpit floor. Presently Thornton helped him lift Harris's body on to it, and they carried what looked like lumps of iron ballast from the stern and put them in the parcel, and them they wrapped the whole thing up like a mummmy and roped it tight, and took one end each. A moment later we heard a faint splash as it went over the side of the boat.

It was all gruesomely businesslike and efficient. Afterwards, Mellor took a bucket and a mop and swabbed down the cockpit, while Thornton stood by with a torch. There must have been a lot of blood, because it took them quite a while to clear up. Once, Thornton looked into the saloon and said, "Okay, Tony?" and Blake said "Yes." Otherwise there wasn't much talking not till they'd finished. Then Thornton and Mellor came back into the saloon.

"Right," said Thornton, "now let's have that drink."

Chapter Nineteen

We had a ghastly night. The few hours left till dawn seemed interminable. The shock of Harris's cold-blooded killing, the callously efficient way in which his body had been disposed of, weighed on us like lead. The certainty that, short of a miracle, a similar fate was in store for us weighed even more heavily, and there was nothing to divert our minds from the grim prospect. I certainly couldn't have cared less at that moment about the story that we'd taken such idiotic risks to get. Neither of us had any great desire to discuss the part that Harris had played in it. There was only one question of interest for the time being, and that was whether we could do anything about our situation. Sitting close together on Mollie's bunk, and talking in whispers, we considered such possibilities as there were—but none offered any real hope. The three men in the saloon were so utterly committed that any one of them would shoot us without a second thought. Another quarrel among them was too much to look for. If there were a sudden, violent change in the weather it might disturb or delay their purpose, perhaps, but the weather seemed as settled as it had been all week. No miracle was likely from that quarter. We talked round and round the problem, and got nowhere.

Sleep, of course, was out of the question. I kept a pretty constant eye on the saloon, just in case some unexpected opportunity should arise—but they were taking no chances. Through the four or five hours till daylight, they mounted an hourly watch. While two of them dozed, or appeared to doze, one sat upright in the lighted saloon with a gun in his lap. Once, during a change-over, Mollie asked for water, and Blake passed some in in a plastic beaker. There was no sadism in any of them; they would dispatch us, I felt sure, when the convenient moment came, with neither pleasure nor pain. We were in the way, and that was all there was to it. It was a situation that left us no room for manoeuvre. We had nothing to offer, nothing to bargain with. On any dispassionate view, we were as good as dead.

Dawn began to break around five and soon they were all on the move. Through the crack in the panel, I could see Mellor lighting the galley stove and starting to make coffee. When it was ready, Blake passed some in to us, with a couple of hunks of bread and butter. He didn't talk to us, and neither did anyone else. They weren't even talking much among themselves. Whatever plans they had were already made, and their only concern was to carry them out smoothly and get away.

As soon as it was full daylight, Thornton and Blake prepared for their dive. We saw them examining the aqualungs, making sure no harm had come to them during the saloon fight, testing the masks. Blake remarked that conditions should be good. I looked out of the port-hole, and the sea was as smooth as pewter. The tide was falling. The cliffs were deserted. We watched the two men strap on their aqualungs and check the pressure gauges and I heard Thornton say that he had enough air for about forty minutes. Then they adjusted their masks and went out into the cockpit and climbed overboard. By the time *Curlew* had swung on her chain sufficiently for us to get a view from the porthole, they'd disappeared in a swirl of bubbles.

Mollie said, in a low voice, "It's now or never, isn't it?"

She was right, of course. If we couldn't turn the tables while we were alone in the boat with Mellor, we certainly couldn't hope to do it when the others got back. But the same thought had obviously occurred to Mellor. Through the crack, I saw that he'd taken up his position on one of the berths in the saloon and was facing us, his finger resting lightly on the trigger of his gun.

Apparently he could see me, too. "Relax, Curtis," he he said quietly, "you haven't a chance. The moment you push on that door I shall shoot you both."

"If you don't shoot us now," I said, "someone will later. What's the odds?"

"Life is sweet," he said. "Why hasten things?"

I moved back a little and whispered to Mollie, "The door opens outwards—there's just a chance I could rush him. I think it's the only hope."

"No!" she said. "No—wait! If only we could distract his attention in some way!"

"I could tell him some people have come to the beach for a swim," I said. "He probably wouldn't believe it, but he'd have to look . . ."

"It's too dangerous—it wouldn't take him a moment . . ."

"Thornton wasn't very quick on the trigger last night," I said.

"No, but I'm sure Mellor is . . . We need something that will really worry him." She gazed agitatedly around. "What about setting fire to the mattresses?"

I lifted one of them, and examined it. It was stuffed with flock. If we *could* set it alight, which I doubted, it would smoke like a bonfire. I shook my head. "It would worry us much more—if he didn't shoot us, we'd suffocate."

"Yes, you're probably right . . . But there must be some way of taking his mind off us." She continued to gaze around. "I suppose there's no way of letting water into the boat, is there?"

I looked at her for a moment. Then I got up and went forward into the toilet compartment. I shut the door behind me in case Mellor was peering through the crack, and took a quick glance round. I'd once known a boat where there was a seacock in the toilet. But there wasn't one here. I got down on my knees and examined the water inlet pipe. If I could get that loose it wouldn't be long before the boat began to fill. Mellor would probably realise what had happened, of course, and come in and plug the hole. But he might not—there were plenty of other places where a leak might start. In any case, his attention would certainly be diverted when water began to lap around his feet. If he thought there was any danger of the boat sinking and leaving him without an escape route, he might hesitate to shoot us. It seemed worth a try. I grasped the pipe with both hands and wedged my foot against the side of the ship and heaved with all my strength. Cracks appeared in the white paint and the gland at the point of entry began to weep slightly. I heaved again, straining every muscle, hoping the whole thing would come away in my hands—but I couldn't move it any more. I gave one more heave, without success, and then went back into the cabin.

"There's a pipe I could loosen if I had some tools," I whispered, "but I can't do anything without . . ."

Mollie looked round blankly. We'd already searched the cabin, and we knew there was nothing. Then she suddenly said, "What's in that little cupboard—we didn't look there," and pointed through the toilet to the forepeak.

I shook my head. "They wouldn't keep anything there—it's the chain locker." All the same, I went and had a look. There weren't any tools. There wasn't anything except the end of the galvanised anchor chain where it joined the bitts. The whole of the chain was out—and, with surprise, I saw that the few feet between the bitts and the hawse hole were quite taut. It looked as though whoever had anchored the boat the evening before had just let the chain run out to the end without bothering to take a turn round the capstan post on neck. There'd probably been a bit of a flap, of course, with our bubbles showing on the water and Mellor signalling from the shore . . .

With quickening pulse, I examined the chain where it joined the bitts. Sometimes chains were made fast, so that the anchor couldn't be slipped. Sometimes they weren't. This one wasn't. The last link was looped over an iron hook in the capstan post, and the chain was tied to the post with a length of strong line. That was all—and I thought I could get it free.

I motioned Mollie to stay outside, and pushed the door shut again, and began to work on the knot: It had been tied a long time, and was very stiff, and though I broke my nails on it I couldn't loosen it at all. If only, I thought, they hadn't taken my knife away . . .! After a moment I stock my head out of the door and beckoned Mollie. "Have you got anything in your bag I can cut with?" I whispered.

She fetched the bag and opened it, and began to go go through the contents. "Is a nail file any good?"

"Better than nothing."

"Or a mirror?"

"That's better still!" I took the little rectangle from her and put it on the floor and tapped it gently with my heel. One of the broken pieces had a good cutting edge, and in a matter of seconds I'd cut through the line. It came apart then very easily. I unwound it until there was nothing holding the end of the chain but the hook. The tension was too tight for me to lift the link off the hook. I put my hand up near the hawse hole and heaved gently on the chain and pulled it in, an inch at a time. If there'd been any wind or tide to speak of outside I'd never have been able to do it, but in a near calm it was only the weight of the chain itself that kept it taut and I had no difficulty with it. When I'd pulled in about six inches I lifted the link off the hook and let the chain go free.

For a moment, the end of it just hung down in the chain locker. Then, link by link, it began to slip through the hawse-hole. It made much more noise going out than it had when I'd slowly pulled it in, and the noise lasted longer. Each link seemed to take an age slipping through and there was nothing I could do to hurry it. Then grating was frightful in my ears—and not only in mine. Suddenly the cabin door burst open and Mellor looked in, the gun pointing at us. He took in the situation in a flash. I was all set to exploit any slip he made, but he didn't make one—he kept out of reach, and the gun didn't waver. "On to that bunks, both of you!" he shouted. "Quick!"

He jerked the gun at Mollie, and she slid on to the bunk.

I lay down beside her. Mellor edged past us, still covering us, still out of reach, to the chain locker. But he was too late. As he got to it, the last few links of the chain ran out with a rush, and I heard the splash as they went into the sea.

Mellor turned on us savagely. The look on his face wasn't in the least debonair now. In fact, I thought he was going to kill us out of hand.

I said, "You're adrift, Mellor. If you shoot us now, you may land up somewhere you don't want to be with the bodies of two people you've *personally* killed. You wouldn't want that, would you?"

For a second, he hesitated. Then he said, "Stay where you are!" and rushed out.

I sat up and looked out of the porthole. We hadn't moved far, but we'd moved. The bubbles over the wreck of *Mary Ann* were ten yards away on the landward side. We were drifting very slowly out of the cove.

I peered through the cracked panel again. Mellor had gone through into the cockpit, closing the outer door of the saloon behind him. Suddenly I heard the whirr of the electric starter as he tried to get the engine going. It whirred for several seconds, but the engine didn't start. Mellor, of course, wasn't familiar with it—and marine engines are notoriously temperamental. I heard him remove the wooden cover. I slipped my shoes off and opened the cabin door. Mollie said "Careful!" and I nodded. I crept silently across to the saloon door. There was a revolving ventilator in one of the panels, partly open, and I looked through it. Mellor was kneeling on the boards, his left hand fiddling with the carburettor, his right still holding the gun. He kept glancing up at the door as he worked. In an interval between glances I gently tried the handle—but he'd locked the door behind him. I could probably break it open, as I'd broken open the other, but he'd still be able to shoot me before I could rush him.

Then I remembered the second gun. Thornton obviously hadn't dived with it, so it must be still aboard *Curlew*. Perhaps he'd left it in his jacket. I looked quickly round the saloon and spotted the jacket hanging from a peg and went through the pockets. But there was no gun. I tried the trousers. Still no gun. He might have put it in one of the cockpit lockers, of course, for safety—or given it to Mellor to take care of . . . I just didn't knowl. Feverishly I picked up Blake's coat and searched that . . . Then my eye fell on the harpoon guns, stowed lengthways at the back of one of the berths.

The starter whirred again. The engine sprang to life, ran for a few seconds, coughed, and died. I picked up one of the harpoon guns and slipped the harpoon in the muzzle and loaded the gun against the floor the way I'd seen it done at Fox's place. Then I crept back to the door. Mellor was bending over the engine again. I poked the harpoon an inch or so through the ventilator slit and held it there. I had to stand so far away from the door to do it that it was difficult to line up the target, but I couln't afford to be fussy. Mellor was getting up to try the starter again. I aimed at his right shoulder, and pressed the trigger.

I missed him completely. I saw the harpoon flash by him and bury its head in the after bulkhead. But the harpoon line, snaking in its wake, looped itself over his right hand, and as I jerked back and pulled it taut his automatic clattered from his grasp into the bilge.

I dropped the harpoon gun and hurled myself against the door. It burst open and I rushed out. Mellor was just retrieving the gun from under the engine. I flung myself at him, and as we both fell with a crash on to the boards the gun flew up into the air in a graceful parabola and dropped into the sea.

We fought with all we had, then, and a bloody business it was. Mellor was no weakling, and he knew all the tricks. As for me, I'd been spoiling for this chance for hours, and I fairly tore into him. As we rolled and jabbed and punched, splinters from the deck gouged into our hands and knees, and sharp edges of seat and bulkhead and engine cover threatened us impartially with sudden and final disaster. Once Mellor broke loose and ripped the harpoon from the wood where it had lodged and came at me with it, holding it like a spear. I dived for his legs and he made a wild stab at me as he went down and missed me by millimetres. I grabbed the harpoon and clung on to it, and for a moment or two we were completely tangled up in the line, Then I landed a lucky blow on his ear and tore myself away from him, and as he staggered up I caught him flush on the chin with a left that had all my weight behind it. His head jerked back, and he dropped like a log.

I drew a deep breath, and looked around for Mollie. She was standing by the saloon door her face white. I could well imagine it had been worse for her than for me. She said, "Oh, Hugh!—are you all right?" in the sort of tone I could have borne to hear oftener from her.

"I'm fine," I said, "I think!" I glanced around the cove. *Curlew* was still drifting slowly out towards the open sea. There was no sign of the divers. We were quite safe. I pulled a silver of wood from the back of my hand and stanched the blood with a handkerchief and Mollie tied it up for me.

"See if you can find some rope," I said, as she finished. "I'll watch Mellor."

She looked in several lockers and finally found a whole coil. Mellor was just beginning to come round, but there wasn't any fight left in him. We lashed him up and half dragged, half carried him into the saloon, and dumped him on one of the bunks. I checked through his pockets to see if he had Thornton's gun on him, but he hadn't.

Next I set to work to get the engine started. It was a four-cylinder job, of a make I'd never handled, but I didn't think there could be much wrong with it. I fiddled a bit with the throttle and choke, but it still wouldn't go. Then I found a plug spanner, and cleaned the plugs, and when I'd put them back it fired at the first touch of the starter and ran perfectly.

"Now what?" Mollie said.

I hesitated, scanning the cove. At any moment, Thornton and Blake would be surfacing. We certainly couldn't risk taking them back on board, but I didn't want to lose sight of them, either.

I said, "I think you'd better take the dinghy ashore and fetch the police. I'll stooge around and try and keep an eye on the other two when they come up. Okay?"

"Okay," she said. That was one thing about Mollie—she was always ready enough to talk me into trouble, but at least she never argued in a crisis.

I put the gear in and headed the boat back into the cove. I steered for a point midway along the beach and shut the engine off just before we reached the shallows. As we lost way, Mollie hauled in the towed dinghy and prepared to climb aboard. At that moment. I saw a masked face break the surface about thirty yards away.

"Quick!" I cried. "They're up."

She clambered nimbly over the stern and dropped into the dinghy and I cast her off. "Better bring plenty of chaps!" I called. "There may be quite a hunt."

"I will," she said. "Look after yourself."

I turned and saw that the divers had submerged again. They'd obviously spotted us, and realised what had happened. I wondered what they'd do next. They certainly couldn't hope to recapture the boat—with the ladder up, they wouldn't even be able to climb aboard. They couldn't hope to throw me off their track by swimming out to sea, because of the bubbles they'd leave—and in any case their air must be almost exhausted. Probably they were already making for the shore. I opened up the engine and steered round the edge of the cove. Almost at once I saw their bubbles. They *were* swimming in—but they were still well to seaward of me. I slowed the boat and waited. They were coming straight for me. Then one of them surfaced again—Blake, I thought. He took a quick look in my direction, and immediately dived. At once they changed their course, swimming parallel to the beach and abreast of me. They seemed to be making for the rocks that formed one of the horns of the cove. I couldn't understand why they were so reluctant to land anywhere near me, considering that they were two to one—and then I suddenly realised. No doubt they thought I had Mellor's gun. I wished I had.

I followed them slowly. I didn't much like the look of the water I was getting into—it was very shallow, and I could see the dark outlines of underwater rocks not far below the surface. But I wanted to keep them in view as long as I could. I stood out a little, and put the gear into neutral, and watched the two bubble lines turn in towards the shore.

Suddenly they surfaced again, almost at the tip of the promontory that divided Curlew Cove from the next one. This time there was no doubt about their intentions. They threw off their aqualungs and shed their masks and flippers and clambered quickly ashore over the low-tide rocks. I put the engine to full ahead and turned

Curlew in to the beach and in a few seconds she ran aground in three or four feet of water.

I needed a weapon badly, now, but I couldn't stop to search the boat for Thornton's automatic and I doubted if Mellor would tell me where it was without more physical persuasion than I was prepared to use. For lack of anything better, I grabbed the second harpoon gun from the bunk in the saloon. Then I dropped overboard and scrambled ashore.

The two men were already out of sight. I loaded the gun, and set off after them over the rocks. It was tricky going, even where the ground was dry, and when I was forced down below high-water mark by steep, encroaching cliffs it became even more treacherous. I had to pick my way over slippery, weed-covered boulders, watching every step. I was constantly worried, too, by the possibility that Thornton and Blake might be lying in wait for me behind some pile of granite. In the open, they would hardly dare come nearer to the gun than forty or fifty feet, but there were splendid opportunities for ambush and the harpoon gun wasn't exactly a handy weapon. I decided to play it safe and moved forward slowly, making quite sure that my flank was cleared before each fresh advance.

The promontory was a wide one, and it took me a full quarter of an hour of rough going before I had a clear view across the mouth of the next cove. I quite expected to see the two men already across it and negotiating the horn on the farther side, but there was no sign of them. Indeed, judging by the way the sea was surging against the base of the cliffs there, there was no way round short of swimming—and I doubted if they'd have wanted to swim again if they could help it. It seemed more likely that they'd turned up into the cove.

I was on better rock now, and making much faster progress. The boulders were smaller, with no cover, and I didn't have to worry any more about ambushes, or the possibility that the men might have doubled back. Steadily I made my way round the foot of the cliff into the cove. Then I saw them, close under the rock at the head of the beach. And I saw something else. As I gazed up at the towering walls, I suddenly realised that this was the place Mollie and I had looked down on from above. It was Hell's Mouth—the cove without an exit. Thornton and Blake, without realising it, had walked into a trap.

I stopped and watched them. By now, they seemed well aware of their danger. Blake was pointing up a one bit of the two-hundred-foot cliff; Thornton at another. They were obviously seeking a track. I moved a little closer in, and stopped again. I didn't want to force things. They must know by now that I hadn't got the automatic, I wouldn't have burdened myself with the harpoon gun. If I went near enough to them to shoot, they'd rush me, and one of them at least would get away. If I stayed where I was, I thought they'd be very reluctant to come within range of the harpoon.

And so, clearly, they were. They kept looking up at the cliff, and back at the sea, seeking some way out. I thought they might split up and try to make a dash past me to the water, but the cove was very narrow; with little room for manoeuvre, and the harpoon evidently deterred them. In the end, they chose the cliff. There must have been some track that I couldn't see, for suddenly Thornton was a dozen feet up and Blake was right on his heels. They were going fast, too. I closed in quickly, but by the time I'd crossed the rough debris at the foot of the cliff they were at extreme range. I hesitated whether to loose a harpoon at Blake on the off-chance of a hit, and decided not to. As I gazed up at the forbidding rock face, serrated enough at the bottom but smoothing out almost immediately above the climbers' heads, it seemed to me that they'd soon be in quite enough trouble without my intervention. For one thing, they were barefoot, which would put a terrific strain on the muscles of their feet; for another, they must already be very tired after their long underwater swim. And Blake had scarcely the build for climbing. In fact, I simply didn't believe they would get far. Better, I thought, to keep the harpoon for when they changed their minds and came down again! I sat down on a boulder, and watched them.

Chapter Twenty

As they moved steadily up towards the half-way mark, to began to dawn on me that I'd seriously underrated them. I'd expected them to become increasingly worried by the height, as almost any novice would be; to show signs of getting stuck at the first difficult pitch. But they didn't. In fact they gave every indication of being pretty skilful rock climbers—especially Thornton. He was still in the lead, climbing with a nice flowing motion, stopping only to reconnoitre for the next footholds and handholds before he moved on. Blake, not far below, was using the same holds and going well. Their progress amazed me. I'd done quite a lot of climbing myself, but this ascent was something I wouldn't have dreamed of tackling without nailed boots and a rope. I could only suppose that like many climbs, it offered more at close quarters than it appeared to do from a distance. From where I sat, some of the pitches above Thornton looked absolutely bare of holds. Yet both men seemed confident.

I began to wonder if I'd been wise to stay on in the cove. At the rate they were going, they'd reach the top long before the police could get to the cliff. What they'd do then, with no clothes but the swimming trunks they were wearing, and no money, was anybody's guess, but they'd never lacked initiative and they were desperate. They might cause a great deal of trouble before they were caught. They might even kill again to get what they needed. I ought to have retraced my steps when they'd started to climb, I told myself, and gone round to the clifftop so that I could intercept them. But it was too late now. The trip back over the weedy rocks to Curlew Cove would take so long that before I could gain the top of Hell's. Mouth they'd either have succeeded or failed—got clear away, or become hopelessly stuck. I might just as well stay where I was.

I continued to watch them. Thornton was already, three-quarters of the way up, and by now I felt certain they'd make it. Another five or ten minutes would see them at the top ... Then, little by little, the picture changed. Thornton had slowed down quite a bit. Once I saw him lower his left foot and wiggle his toes in the air as though he was trying to ease a touch of cramp. He took another step, and then he stopped again. There was a patch of lighter rock ahead of him, which from the ground had a shaly appearance. I saw him staring up at it, examining it carefully. Then he looked to his right and left. He didn't seem very happy about things. After a moment he abandoned the straight ascent and began a hand traverse to his left.

Blake was three or four yards below him, now, and going even more slowly. He seemed to be worried by his feet too. Once he hung by his hands for a full minute, letting his legs dangle. When he resumed the climb he looked much less confident. Thornton had left him too far behind which meant that from now on he'd got to find his own holds. Gradually, his route diverged from Thornton's. He moved up a few more feet. Suddenly a piece of rock came clattering to the ground in a shower of small stones, as one of his footholds gave way. He recovered himself all right, but his nerve seemed shaken. He no longer had the appearance of an expert, and I began to have serious doubts about him. He was directly below what looked to me like a slight overhang, and he didn't seem to know how to negotiate it. He looked to the right and the left, as Thornton had done under the shale. He tried for a hold with his right foot, and drew back. He tried for another with his left, but he couldn't quite reach it. Then he took a step that made me draw my breath in sharply. He'd done a thing that no climber should ever do. He'd crossed his legs!

I'll never forget the tense horror of those next few minutes. Whatever was coming to Blake was no more, I supposed, than his deserts, yet I'd done enough climbing not to wish any man in a predicament like this. For now he seemed paralysed. His right arm was fully extended above his head in a position that he couldn't possibly maintain for long. His left hand had no more than a steadying hold. His feet were hopelessly tangled. If he could have raised himself a little he might have got free, but presumably his right hand-hold wasn't good enough. Anyway, he didn't do it. He just clung there. Presently he gave a shout—an agonised "Help!" that echoed among the rocks and set the gulls wheeling around him. Thornton, who had finished his traverse, glanced down. Blake shouted again. Thornton took in the situation—and continued his climb. Not that there was anything Thornton could have done for his companion—the only thing that could help Blake now was a rope from above and a rescuer.

Perhaps that was what he hoped for—but he hadn't a chance. No rescuer could have got down in time, even if there'd been one around. His shouts grew wilder. I guessed that his arm was growing cramped and that he knew he couldn't hold on. I retreated from under the cliff face, sick with suspense.

The end came suddenly. Blake's right arm relaxed its grip and his hand slithered down the rock, scrabbling for a fresh hold. It didn't find any. He glanced, down, swayed away from the cliff, and gave a hideous yell. The next moment his pink body came hurtling down to the boulders a hundred feet below. He hit the ground with a dull smack, writhed once or twice, and lay still in a twisted heap. I went over to him, but there was nothing I could do. His skull was crushed in, and he was quite dead.

The sight must have shaken Thornton, for momentarily he had stopped climbing. He still had about twenty feet to go to the top, and it wasn't an easy pitch. I stepped back again, well clear of the cliff's base, in case he didn't make it. Then, as I looked up, I suddenly saw something move above him. There was someone on the clifftop. I backed towards the sea, to widen the angle and show myself, and a man turned a pair of glasses on me and then waved. I waved back—it was a policeman in a flat cap. Then Mollie appeared beside him, and another man. I kept pointing to the face of the rock, and cupped my hands and shouted that Thornton was climbing. I doubted if they could hear but someone got the right idea because one of the men lay down at the edge of the precipice and peered over. As he did so, Thornton looked up, and stopped.

I hardly needed telling what would happen next. Thornton had three deaths on what, with any other man, would have been his conscience. He had personally committed two cold-blooded murders. There'd be no mercy for him—he hadn't a hope. Seeing the police above him, he must know he hadn't a hope. There was only one reasonable thing he could do—let go!

I waited for it. I was glad I couldn't see his face. I got as far away from the cliff as I could because I didn't want to hear that ghastly crunch again. I saw him lean away from the cliff and look down, once. I braced myself.

Then he continued to climb! He climbed steadily up the last fifteen feet and into the arms of the waiting police. He had plenty of nerve for killing, but not enough for dying. I guess you can never tell with people, till the moment comes.

Chapter Twenty One

Mollie and I didn't hear the full story of the conspiracy until much later that day, after the police had grilled Thornton and Mellor. When we did, this was how it went.

The four men had met during World War II. Thornton and Blake, then in their early twenties and ready for any adventure, had belonged to one of those small, hush-hush units whose job it was to land secretly on enemy coasts, dispose of guards and sentries without fuss, and carry out high-speed demolition work. Cliff climbing and underwater swimming had been part of their training. Mellor and Harris had both been in the Navy, operating small, fast boats, and they'd run into the other two when they'd carried a party across the Channel on a particularly hazardous mission. After the war, contact had been maintained.

The plot had originated with Thornton, who—in partnership with Blake—was already living by his wits under cover of a phoney import-export business that he'd started. The idea had first occurred to him when he'd seen an advertisement for a new captain for Bruce Attwood's yacht. He'd worked out a rough plan for raiding the yacht and grabbing Chairman Attwood's much-publicised jewels, which depended only on Harris getting the job. He'd managed to sell the idea to Harris, with Mellor's persuasive help, and Harris—who had already captained several large private yachts—had applied for the job and got it. Once that key position had been won, the rest had been comparatively straightforward.

Thornton had realised, early on, that whatever boat was used for the raid would have to be described to the police afterwards by Harris, so it was essential that they should use one that didn't implicate any of them. The idea of stealing one locally had been turned down on the obvious ground that it might not be in suitable condition. The alternative was to appear to steal one, from a member of the gang who would have no other role than to seem its innocent owner. Mellor had been cast for that role, and immediately after Harris's appointment to *Wanderer* he'd bought *Mary Ann* and begun to prepare her for the raid. From that moment, he'd avoided any open association with the others. At about the same time, Thornton and Blake had bought *Curlew*, so that when the time came they would have a legitimate reason for hanging about in *Wanderer's* neighbourhood. Mellor, who might well come under some slight suspicion at first, was to arrange a trip to the Continent to cover the period of the raid.

Harris had kept the others informed by telephone of Attwood's plans, so far as he knew them, and when *Wanderer* had moved to Falmouth for the start of her Mediterranean cruise, Mellor had given out that he planned a trip to the Scillies and had taken *Mary Ann* to Cornwall as a first step. Mellor had been something of an artist in building up his front, omitting no corroborative detail, even to his exchanges with his bank. His expressed intention of taking a girl with him had been part of the front, aimed at strengthening the impression of a purely holiday trip. In the event, Gloria Drage had been the least satisfactory part of the façade. She was just one of his casual telephone numbers, and he'd had to make do with her in spite of her glaring deficiencies as a sailing companion because the trip had had to be announced rather hurriedly and none of his other girl friends had been free.

Mellor, while neglecting no outward preparation, had never expected to get as involved over the Scillies trip as he had. The plan had been that Thornton and Blake should return *Mary Ann* to her anchorage in Gillan Creek after the said. The police, it was assumed, would find her almost at once; a letter about insurance, purposely left aboard, would give them the owner's name and address; they would try to get in touch with Mellor and learn that he was in Belgium; and in the end it would be they who would tell *him* about the theft of his boat. They would hear about the holiday he'd planned, and everything would seem perfectly above hoard. Since *Mary Ann* would be important evidence in the case, Mellor would be unable to carry out his projected trip, and would merely ring Gloria and call it off. That had been the plan.

A day or two before the raid, Thornton and Blake had moored *Curlew* in the Falmouth anchorage—close to *Wanderer*, but not too close. They had carefully avoided all contact with the ship and its crew; the necessary information about her, we now discovered, had been conveyed to them in a way so simple that it had never occurred to us. Harris, it appeared, had written his messages on the inside of an empty cigarette packet, which he'd then tossed overboard to float away on the tide at a moment when he saw that Thornton and Blake were observing him. In due course, one of the two men had rowed off in their dinghy and quietly scooped it up. As occasion offered, they'd communicated with Harris in the same way. Actually, I remembered now that I'd been present when Harris had thrown a packet overboard, but naturally I'd thought nothing of it at the time. The method had worked perfectly, and Thornton had been primed, an hour before *Wanderer's* departure, with all details of her sailing time, course and speed. The facts about her cabin arrangement and lay-out had largely been given by Harris earlier, in a letter to Thornton.

The moment Thornton and Blake had received their sailing directions, they'd rowed ashore and left by car for Gillan Creek. They'd parked the car in the bushes, paddled out in Mellor's dinghy to *Mary Ann*, anchored the dinghy, broken into the cabin to give the impression of theft, and at once sailed for the agreed interception point.

No flare had been used, nor had any been necessary. With both ships on the look-out for each other, contact had been made without the slightest difficulty. Harris had reported a flare simply because he had to have some excuse for stopping. The presence of the *Northern Trader* in the vicinity had been an unforeseen factor. Harris had appreciated the danger that the cargo ship might report that she'd seen no flare, but he'd decided that that particular risk must be accepted, since any last-minute change of plan would have involved *Wanderer* in manoeuvres that would have taken a lot of explaining to Quigley, if he'd happened to be awake.

After the interception, everything had gone according to plan—for a while. Thornton and Blake had boarded *Wanderer* with blackened faces. Harris had made a show of resistance, for Quigley's benefit, and received a measured blow on the cheek. Rope for the tying-up was handy. The raiders had then smashed the radio transmitter, shut off the forecastle, and gone below. They'd quickly jammed up the cabin doors with the wedges they'd brought with them, and Blake had gone into Charmian Attwood's cabin to get the jewel case. He'd glanced inside it to make sure the jewels were there, but, as it turned out afterwards, he hadn't shut it up properly. His silence had been no more than an ordinary precaution in case his path and Charmian's should ever cross again.

It was while Blake was in the cabin that things had started to go wrong. David Scott, hearing Charmian's scream and all the row outside in the corridor, had presumably tried to open his door and found he couldn't. He'd looked out of his porthole—this, of course, was all supposition—seen the empty boat tied up alongside, put boat and noise together, and decided that *Wanderer* was being raided. He'd got out his gun—it now appeared that what he'd owned was a heavy Colt—and emptied into the cruiser below the water line. Thornton, hearing the succession of shots, and realising that he couldn't get quickly into Scott's jammed cabin, had emptied his own gun through the cabin door with the intention of disabling Scott and so preventing any further damage to *Mary Ann*. Scott, it was assumed, had dropped the Colt into the sea as he'd fallen back from the porthole to collapse on the floor.

Thornton and Blake, returning to *Mary Ann*, had found her making water at an alarming rate. The engine flywheel had been already half-submerged, and Thornton had feared that if the engine were started the flying spray might short-circuit the ignition. As a temporary measure he'd hoisted the sail to take them clear of *Wanderer*, then both men had set to work to try and plug the holes in the hull. They'd had to break up the starboard bunk with an axe to get at the underwater section, working with feverish haste in cramped surroundings, and it had been during this initial struggle that the jewel case, placed on the table by Blake, had been knocked off into the rapidly rising bilge, scattering its contents. They'd carried on, having much more on their minds just then than jewels, but the water had beaten them. They'd retreated to the cockpit without being able to find the leaks, and Blake had operated the pump while Thornton bailed with a bucket. For a time they'd more than held their own that way, and presently they'd got the engine going and set *Mary Ann* on her course back to Gillan Creek. But all the way back they'd had to go on pumping and bailing and as the hours had passed they'd tired. By the time they were approaching the Helford estuary the water was beating them again, and Thornton had feared that they might founder before they reached their destination. He'd decided the only thing to do was to beach the boat, and they'd turned in to the coast just south of Gillan Creek. They'd managed to make their way into a quiet cove, but before they could get to the beach the flooded engine had died on them. The two men had hurriedly flung all loose objects into the cabin and shut the doors, so that there wouldn't be any flotsam to give the boat's presence away. Then *Mary Ann* had settled under them, and they'd had to swim for it as she sank.

The time had been just before dawn. They'd cleaned up as best they could, and then made their way by track and minor road to Gillan Creek, little more than a mile distant, without meeting anyone. They'd collected their car, driven back to Falmouth, picked up their dinghy, and slipped aboard *Carlew* just as *Wanderer* was returning to the anchorage. They'd changed their clothes, breakfasted, and awaited inquiries.

At low water that day they'd returned to the cove and discovered to their relief that the top of the wreck didn't show and that there was nothing to reveal its presence. It was then that Thornton had decided to try and salvage the jewels by using aqualungs. But they needed help—they needed a third person around who could keep a permanent and inconspicuous watch on the cove, and grab the jewels if the weather should change suddenly during the night and drive *Mary Ann* up the beach. Harris was in no position to do it, so that left Mellor. On the Friday night, Thornton had rung up Mellor at his London lodgings.

Mellor, by then, had been in a bit of a flap. He'd returned from Belgium that afternoon, very surprised that the police hadn't made any effort to get in touch with him. He'd read through the newspaper accounts of the raid and had realised that something had gone very wrong. He'd been in two minds whether to ring up the police himself and say that the boat mentioned in the story sounded like his, or whether to take Gloria down to Cornwall as though the Scillies trip was still on. Thornton, on the phone, had decided the matter for him. He was to go down as though he'd heard nothing, and get all the news when he arrived.

Thornton, meanwhile, had been in communication with Harris by means of the cigarette packets, and had fixed up the Bodmin Moor rendezvous for Mellor. Harris had had no difficulty in passing on the message to Mellor in the course of conversation with him about *Mary Ann* at Gillan Creek. Mellor had subsequently worked up a quarrel with Gloria, to the point where she'd flounced off and returned to London. Next day he'd kept the appointment with Thornton on Bodmin Moor, heard the story of the raid in detail, and received his instructions—to camp on the cliffside within sight of the cove and keep an eye on developments. Then Blake and Thornto had driven into Plymouth and bought some aqualung equipment, and the next day they'd set to work on their salvage operation. It had taken them longer than they'd expected, for they'd had some trouble locating the wreck, and then they'd had to anchor it as a precaution against worsening weather, and in the actula work of recovery they'd been hapered all the time by the dirty bilge water trapped in the cabin—as well as by the need to go off at frequent intervals to get their bottles recharged. But they'd almost finished the job when we'd got on to their track.

That, broadly, was the story. If ever two men deserved the fate that awaited them, Thornton and Mellor did, but I still felt some regret over Harris. Apparently he'd been even more upset about Scott than we'd realised, and he'd sent a bitter message to Thornton about the unplanned shooting, via Mellor. The real trouble with

Harris—apart of course from the fundamental one that he'd been prepared to take part in a criminal raid for money—had been his naïveté. Compared with Thornton and Mellor, and even Blake, he'd been a very simple man, and that had been his undoing.

Chapter Twenty Two

At seven o'clock that evening Mollie and I took the ferry to St. Mawes to be out of the way of the hordes of London reporters who'd be descending on Falmouth again at any moment. We'd phoned our offices, and basked in brief, ecstatic praise. Now we both wanted to relax. We found a pub with an attractive terrace over-looking the water, and I ordered drinks. Mollie was still a little pale after her ordeal, but professionally she was on top of the world. Her only regret was that, by going off to fetch the police, she'd missed the last dramatic episode in the story and hadn't been able to send an eye-witness account of the Death Climb.

"Next time," she said, nibbling a salted almond, "I shall let you go for the police."

I laughed. "There isn't going to be a next time," I said, "not as far as I'm concerned. Two narrow squeaks in three months are quite sufficient for me. I want to live!"

"In that case I suppose I'll have to follow my next hunch on my own."

"Why follow it at all? I still say there's no future for you in all this recketing around."

"But I like racketing around."

"You might like being married to me if you tried it," I said. "You never know."

She considered that. "Yes, I suppose I might, in some ways—but I just don't have the slightest urge to settle down."

"Well, it isn't natural—that's all I can say."

She gave me a delightful smile. "I've plenty of time to be natural," she said.

THE END

www.ingramcontent.com/pod-product-compliance
Ingram Content Group UK Ltd.
Pitfield, Milton Keynes, MK11 3LW, UK
UKHW040105010325
455690UK00002B/14